Under the Black Flag

UNDER THE BLACK FLAG

by Erik Christian Haugaard

ROBERTS RINEHART PUBLISHERS

For the captain and the crew of the *Pipedream*

Published in the United States of America by
Roberts Rinehart Publishers
Post Office Box 666, Niwot, Colorado 80544

Published in Ireland by
Roberts Rinehart Publishers
Trinity House, Charleston Road
Ranelaigh, Dublin 6, Republic of Ireland

Distributed in the U.S. and Canada by Publishers Group West

Second Printing January 1995

ISBN 1-879373-63-7
Library of Congress Catalog Card Number 93-85476

Printed in the United States of America
Cover art and text illustrations by Birgitta Saflund

Contents

Preface

IN 1716 THE CARIBBEAN SEA WAS AS FILLED WITH pirates as with sharks, and it is a matter of opinion as to which were the most bloodthirsty. Captain Teach, Blackbeard, was born in Bristol, England; Major Bonnet on the island of Barbados. They were once as real and alive as you. The *Queen Anne's Revenge* is not a ship constructed in my mind, but a vessel that once plowed the waters of the Carolinas, bringing fear to those who sighted it. Gibbens, Owen Roberts, Isreal Hands, and John Husk did once answer to their names.

They were a cruel lot, living in cruel times, when the life of a human being had little value. The sailor gambled with death, and death most often won. The temptation to become a pirate was great. Riches almost beyond their imagination could be theirs. Was not the Governor of Jamaica, Sir Henry Morgan, once the pirate Henry Morgan? All pirates knew the story of that scoundrel, knighted and honored by his king. Those not so lucky ended up in the gallows or begging in the streets of London.

I owe much to Daniel Defoe, Captain Charles Johnson, and that amazing literary buccaneer, Alexander Exquemelin. For the tale of Hugo Peachel I am indebted to Dr. Paul Reese, who dug it out of a Hamburg newspaper printed in 1670.

That is enough. Come on board, the canvas is unfurled, let us sail!

Chapter 1

Our ship is captured by pirates and I am taken hostage

"*A SHIP TEN DEGREES TO STARBOARD, KEEPING*
our course." The young mate handed his telescope to our captain.
"I think she is a brigantine, sir."

"The young man thinks. Uncommon among officers these
days." The captain put the glass to his eye and looked aft. "He is
right, too. She is a brigantine and probably manned by brigands
as well. She is carrying all the canvas she can muster. Would you
care to have a look?" He handed the telescope to a fat merchant
from Jamaica who had taken passage to London. "Let go the royals," he then ordered.

I looked at the sailors, who on command climbed the rigging
as agile as monkeys, and envied them. When I had tried to climb,
the captain had ordered me down, saying that I was a passenger
and that he was responsible for me.

I didn't care for the captain or the fat merchant, though the
captain was always very polite to me in spite of my being only a
boy. This was not so surprising as the ship he commanded was

1

owned by my father. She was three masted but very slow, especially now when fully loaded.

I turned and looked forward. The endless sea stretched to the horizon. Somewhere far beyond what my eyes could see was a country called England, and for that our course was set. When my father talked about that country his eyes would grow moist, but mine would not. I was being sent there, my father had said, "to learn to be a gentleman."

But I had no desire for such schooling. I was fourteen years old and still more boy than man. I loved Jamaica and had no wish to exchange it for that fog-bound island.

With a loud crack the royals unfurled and were set. I looked aft at the ship pursuing us. It was clearly visible now.

"Will it catch us?" the fat merchant asked, his voice trembling with fear.

"If she does, we shall give her a warm welcome."

The captain glanced complacently at the sixteen guns displayed on deck. They were five-pounders. Then he gave an order for a spritsail to be rigged.

"What flag does she fly?" The merchant turned to the mate who had again put the telescope to his eye.

"None at present." The mate grinned. "They don't usually haul up their black rag until they are within firing distance."

"A pirate?" The merchant was twisting a gold ring on his finger. A reply was unnecessary for at that moment the captain gave orders to unlash the guns and to bring powder and cannonballs on deck.

I stared at the brigantine pursuing us. She was fast, carrying much sail, and the light wind was in her favor.

"A pirate," I whispered. I was not afraid, and though I had heard many stories of pirates' cruelty, the word still had a aura of romance for me.

"Give out weapons to the crew," the captain ordered and

turning to the merchant, he asked with a sneer if he could handle a gun. The merchant shook his head, no, and the captain suggested that he go below. Seeing me, he aked, "What about you, Will? Are you going to fight or should I send you below, too?"

That was the first time the captain had used that common shortening of my name, William. I answered that I was thought a fair shot, and that I would prefer to stay on deck.

I was given a pistol that looked as if it had been stored in salt water. I cleaned it as best I could, loaded it, cocked it, and put powder in the pan. I fired in the general direction of the pirate ship, but all that happened was a flash in the pan as the charge did not ignite. A sailor near me grinned, and I handed the useless pistol to him.

The brigantine was now close enough to fire at us. It carried only eight guns, but they were nine-pounders. Their shots hit the sea in our wake, sending up a great spray. Then they hauled up a black flag, flying it from their mizzenmast. As it rose the pirates cheered and fired another salvo at us.

We were not hit, but this time one of the shots landed close to our stern. The captain gave orders for our guns to answer, but being only five-pounders their charge was too light, and the cannonballs fell miserably short. Now the pirates turned about, and keeping carefully out of range, they came up on our larboard side and fired once more. Luck, I guessed, rather than great gunnery, helped one of their cannonballs hit our main topmast, sending it, sails and all, down upon our deck and into the water.

Our ship swerved out of control and went into the wind. The sail on the foremast backed, and for a moment I feared that it, too, would go overboard. The mate ran forward with an axe, ready to cut the fallen rigging and free us of the wreckage, and the captain gave orders to furl the sails and strike our colors. As our flag came down great cheers were heard from the pirate brigantine, and their sailors climbed the riggings and furled their sail as well.

Our sailors were busy saving as much of the sails and rigging as they could.

"They are good sailors." The captain was standing close to me.

"I tell you, Will, most of them have served in His Majesty's ships and learned their trade well. Now we must see what kind of bargain we can strike with them. Gold for our lives."

"Will they kill us?" The merchant had come on deck again while the pirates were lowering a boat and manning it.

"They might. Depends on who is their captain, but they are not cannibals." The captain looked at the merchant then suddenly recalling that the man had paid for his passage to England he said, "If they leave us the ship, we shall be running back to Jamaica for repairs, sir."

Home, I thought, and in my mind's eye I saw again our house, the largest and finest on the island, my father claimed. He was proud of it and with good reason. Memory conjured up another picture, of the girl who had been my nurse when I was small.

She was a slave girl, born on my father's plantation, and not many years older than I. She had been as much my companion as my nurse. It had been harder for me to leave her than my mother, a strange, cold woman who hated our island and had only one wish: to return to England where she was born.

When I was small I had been afraid of my mother, not that she had ever done me harm. She had a large room in our house, which she seldom left, taking even her meals there. I would be brought there once a day by my little companion, Mary. My mother would look at me and ask if I was well, a strange question to ask a tiny child. I had quickly learned to say, "Yes, mother." Then she would wave me away and Mary would take me by the hand and lead me back to "our" part of the house.

Thinking that I would soon be back, and how pleased Mary would be, I smiled as I watched the pirates' boat approaching. They rowed well, keeping time. A tall man sat at the tiller.

"Blackbeard," the mate whispered to the captain, who nodded in agreement.

"A precious rogue if there ever was one. But once he has taken what he wants he usually lets the ship go. Captain Teach," our captain hollered, "you have good gunners aboard."

The pirate took off his hat and waved it in reply, then brought his boat alongside our ship. He was the first man up the ladder, and I looked at him with some curiosity, for he was an infamous pirate. His long, black beard was divided into three braids and tied with a ribbon, giving rise, I presumed, to his nickname, Blackbeard. His hair was also long and unruly. His nose was large and his small eyes were so dark that they seemed to be black as well. From his belt dangled three pistols.

His boat crew had now climbed aboard and formed a circle around us on the quarterdeck. I stared at the motley crowd. Some of them were handsomely dressed, others almost clad in rags, but all of them were well armed.

"Captain O'Rourke, we have met before." With a grin, the pirate captain doffed his hat.

"Aye, Captain Teach, but that was when we were both within the law. I hope you will not rob an old shipmate of his command."

"She is too slow for my trade." For the moment the pirate looked back at his own vessel with pride.

"Handsome is as handsome does," our captain grumbled. "But I suppose you will strip us as naked as when we were born."

"That would not be a pretty sight," Captain Teach laughed, and pointing to the fat merchant, asked him what had happened to the ring he usually wore. The merchant looked with dismay at his fingers. On one, a white ring of skin was almost as notice-able as the gold ring had been.

"I left it in the cabin," the merchant mumbled.

"Jim!" Captain Teach pointed to a particularly rascally looking member of his crew who carried a cutlass. "Help this gentleman find his ring. He may also have left his purse in some odd place, and have difficulty finding it." The merchant was about to object but a sharp jab with the cutlass in his rear sent him in the direction of the ladder leading below. His departure was greeted with loud laughter from the pirates and most of our own crew.

Captain Teach turned to our crew. "You have no need of your weapons any more. Gather them together here in front of me," he commanded as he pointed to a spot on the deck not far from the toes of his boots. "Your knives you can keep and your belongings will not be touched by us. We don't steal from brothers." This brought a cheer from our crew as well as the pirates.

He will leave us the ship but our crew might join his and turn pirate, I thought. Blackbeard was known as the cruellest of the pirates that infested our waters, yet now he was behaving as if he had suddenly acquired a heart of gold.

"My compliments, Captain Teach. May I ask if you conduct Sunday school on your vessel as well?" Our captain smiled affably at the pirate.

"My dear Captain O'Rourke, cannot a pirate be a gentleman? Was not Henry Morgan knighted by the king?" Blackbeard's superior smile revealed a set of teeth as black as his beard.

"Yes, Sir Henry was elevated by His Majesty, though not in the manner that most of his enemies would have wished for," our captain grumbled. He did not care for that old pirate who became vice governor of Jamaica, and would have preferred him to have been hanged.

"Save me! Save me!" The fat merchant came running up on deck and threw himself down in front of Blackbeard, his hands folded as if he was praying to the pirate. The man guarding the merchant appeared, grinning behind him, a purse dangling from his hands.

"What's the matter?" The pirate turned to the guard, holding out his hand to receive the purse.

"He claims that this purse contains all the gold he owns. I disagreed with him and we had a small argument." The rascal handed the purse to his captain, who opened it and looked inside.

"By God, Jim, methinks you are right. This is not much to bring to London town." Captain Teach drew his own weapon, a rapier with a rather short blade. Touching the merchant's chin with its point, he forced him to look up. "Methinks that you have forgotten what you did with your money. Now be good enough to remember it, for I do not care to spoil Captain O'Rourke's deck by spilling blood on it."

"Sir, I am owed money in London, therefore I do not need to carry much." The merchant almost wept.

It was not a bad excuse for a light purse, but I did not believe it was the truth anymore than Captain Teach.

"Rise, you money-grubbing cheater of honest men, and let me look at you," Blackbeard shouted, withdrawing his weapon.

The merchant was a pitiful sight, though it was hard for me to feel sorry for him. Suddenly, the pirate lunged with his rapier towards the merchant's belly. I thought blood would be spurting, but he had merely cut the belt that secured the man's trousers and they fell around his ankles. Shouts of merriment came from the pirates and from our crew as well. It appeared that the merchant wore two belts; one to hold up his dignity, the other his wealth. The second belt revealed three purses hanging from it. Another plunge with the rapier and the three bags of gold fell on the deck with a thud. This time the merchant's skin was also cut, and a thin stream of blood ran down his leg. The merchant threw himself upon the deck, hiding his head with his hands.

Blackbeard looked at the coward with the disgust of a man to whom fear is unknown. "You are a dog. Bark!" he ordered. The pirates cheered as the merchant was made to run on all fours along the deck, barking as loudly as he could.

Blackbeard picked up the three purses and examined their content, which he found to his approval. Then he ordered the merchant to be put on a lead and tied to the mizzenmast.

Now began a complete search of our ship. First, our captain and the two mates were told to stay aft by the wheel, and our crew was ordered to the forecastle. Then, anything the pirates desired was brought up on deck and transported to their brigantine. The pirates had no use for our casks of raw sugar, but the fourteen casks of rum were all brought up on deck and dispatched.

When Captain Teach finally decided that nothing remained worth stealing, he presented his compliments to our captain in an elaborate manner, and ordered his crew to man the longboat. Just as he was about to debark he spotted the merchant who was still tied to the mizzenmast and was crouching there. "The dog," he said, and called back two of his men. "I think I shall take him with me," he declared.

"No, no," the merchant begged. Still on all fours, his glance turned beseechingly to Blackbeard. "I have children and a wife," he wailed.

Captain Teach looked thoughtfully at the merchant. "I wonder what they would pay to have you back?"

"They are poor." The merchant crawled towards the pirate's boots as if he was going to lick them. "But there is someone on board whose father would pay his weight in gold to get him back." The merchant raised one finger and pointed it at me. "His father is so rich they call him the king of Jamaica. Why, this very ship is his."

"Is that true?" Blackbeard looked at our captain and then at me.

"It is true that William's father owns my command, but as far as being called the king of Jamaica, that I have never heard of, nor do I know the extent of his wealth. As for the scoundrel here," Captain O'Rourke looked with revulsion at the kneeling merchant, "if you do take him on board your ship, please be kind enough to throw him overboard for me."

"I shall leave that human maggot for you to deal with, but this young princelet might be worth his keep. Bind him and we shall take him on board," he ordered two members of his crew.

"Don't come near me!" I shouted, drawing a little knife that I had hidden in my scarf.

"This puppy bites," Blackbeard laughed. "That is more to my liking. Climb the ladder by yourself and you shall be my guest on board until your father pays for your passage to Jamaica."

I looked at Captain O'Rourke and realized that he could not help me. Then I looked at the merchant dog who was now grinning with relief. "I shall not forget you," I said, and walked to the bulwark where the companion ladder hung. Taking one glance at the ship, I straightened myself and then swung my legs over the planks. Grabbing the ropes of the ladder, I climbed down into the boat below.

"You are a sensible boy." Captain Teach seated himself at the tiller and gave orders for the crew to push off. "Courage is great, but without sensibility, it is worthless." The crew pulled smartly on the oars, and the longboat shot towards the brigantine. I looked back at our ship. It had drifted stern towards us and I could read its name, *Sarah Rose*, my mother's name, and its home port, *Kingston*. I wondered if I should ever see either again.

Chapter 2

Isreal Hands

TWO WEEKS HAD GONE BY SINCE I HAD BECOME Blackbeard's prisoner. The pirate had shown a strange liking for me and kept me constantly at his side. I had been allowed keep my knife, my clothes, and even the gold cross and chain that I wore around my neck.

He liked to talk to me, I thought. Or was he merely talking to himself? No man among his crew was his friend. He preferred some to others, but trusted none.

"Only on the sea is a man free. You will learn the truth of this, princeling." Captain Teach liked the title he had coined for me. "On shore you are whatever others call you, you dance to their tunes, but here you can be king. Here no one cares where your cradle stood, but only what you are." I nodded in agreement, though I felt far from sure that this was true.

"Captain O'Rourke and I sailed together. That was when the war was still on and any French ship on the sea was yours if you could take it. O'Rouge, I used to call him. He was never one to be shy when boarding. He was quartermaster then, and knew more than north from south." Captain Teach smiled as he thought of bygone times. "While I stayed in the forcastle, he was made an officer, so we each sailed a different course. He is a good seaman. Your father did well by giving him a command."

Again I nodded to indicate agreement.

"Ship in the offing," a voice sang out from the crow's-nest.

"Where?" Blackbeard bellowed, glancing up at the lookout.

"Twenty degrees to larboard...she is a big one," the sailor shouted back.

"How many masts and what is her course?" The pirate's small eyes were shining.

He doesn't care about the gold, it is the fight he longs for, I thought.

"Three-masted. She is light, carrying but little cargo. As for her course, as near as I can make out it is the opposite of ours." By now most of the crew were staring in the direction the look-out had given.

"Princeling, run to my cabin and bring me my glass." Captain Teach gave me a helpful push in the direction of the companion-way. In his cabin, I recognized the telescope that was lying on top of a chart on the table. It had belonged to Captain O'Rourke. I looked at the engraved name on the brass instrument. Jonathan Bernard, my father.

"Aye, she is big and carries a goodly amount of guns. Let us hope there are none on board who know how to use them." Blackbeard turned to me. "Keep a sharp eye on her and tell me if she changes course. Princeling, soon we shall know if you have blood or water in your veins."

"I will not fight, sir. I am your prisoner, not a member of your crew."

"Maybe I shall tie you to the mast, so you cannot run away to hide or dodge the lead. What say you to that?"

"I am your prisoner," I repeated. "A prisoner has no choice but to obey his captor. You can tie me to your mast if you care to."

"Maybe I will." Captain Teach peered into his telescope again, mumbling to himself. "Built somewhat like a frigate, yet not a frigate, no man of war, yet well armed. A prize worth the taking—and keeping." Turning, he called out for Isreal Hands.

I knew the pirate he was shouting for. He was a strange fellow who, usually after drinking too much rum, would pray loudly and fervently. His shipmates paid little attention to this, which made me certain that it was a common performance no longer found interesting enought to comment upon.

"Take charge of the princeling," the captain said. "Keep him on deck and tell me later how well he stood up when the bullets sang." Isreal Hands put his hand on my shoulder and guided me towards the forecastle. The pirates were already getting the guns ready middeck, and we would be in the way.

"Now why would the captain call you princeling?" Isreal Hands asked, seating himself on the aft part of the bowsprit.

"I don't know ... maybe because he thinks it a joke. My name is William Bernard. I come from Jamaica."

"And is your father a pirate, too?" Isreal Hands looked dreamily at the approaching ship. "They come to a bad end, you know."

"My father owns a plantation. He is not a pirate. But if you know they come to a bad end, why are you a pirate?" I asked, a little shocked at the idea of my father being a pirate.

Isreal Hands pointed in the general direction of his heart, "Inside me there are two people. One is a pirate and the other is a preacher of the Lord. When one is hanged, the other can say his prayers for him."

The foreign ship was now close enough for us to make out her colors. She seemed to be flying the Spanish flag. "Antichrist," the pirate whispered as if telling me a secret.

"It is Spanish." I said.

"Are they not antichrist with their heathen images that they worship?" The pirate drew his cutlass from his belt.

"Most of the people on Jamaica are Catholic, and the image they worship is the Blessed Virgin."

"You must not make graven images. Does it not say so in the Book?" Isreal Hands looked severely at me. I shrugged my shoulders. I did not feel up to arguing about religion.

As I looked aft, to my surprise I saw the flag of Spain flying from the gaff of our mizzenmast as well. "We are flying the same colors," I said pointing to the flag.

"It is but a ruse." The pirate's smile was crafty. The two ships were passing very close to each other.

A lookout in the bow waved to us, and Isreal Hands sprang up and waved back. I saw that our sailors were ready to fire all nine-pounders on our larboard side. The cannons had not been loaded with cannonballs but with scraps of iron, nails, and whatever could be found for the destruction of the sailors on the other ship. As we passed we fired. Even standing in the bow I could see the carnage caused by our broadside. The powder smoke had not cleared from our decks before I heard Captain Teach order "About ship," in a loud voice. The jib and staysail fluttered for a moment, then filled again as the brigantine set on the new course.

Again we approached the unlucky Spanish ship, and our port guns caused more slaughter as we passed it. The Spanish ship's helmsman had been killed and the ship swerved onto our course, almost ramming us, and then went into the wind. I had not noticed that our longboat had been put into the water, but now it cast off and headed for the Spanish prize.

I could not help admiring Blackbeard's seamanship. If England had still been at war, could he not have ended up like that famous buccaneer, Henry Morgan, knighted by the king, and dying rich in his bed? Certainly, he was an excellent sailor who drove his ship as if it was a part of him.

Again the order "about ship" was shouted, not by Captain Teach, but by his boatswain, Mr. Gibbens—or Gibbet as he was usually called. Blackbeard was in the longboat alongside the Spaniard. Grappeling irons were thrown up, and as our ship went into the wind I could see the pirates boarding the prize. The fight was not long, and soon the Spanish colors were struck.

When its colors came down, Isreal Hands waved his cutlass in the air and screamed a loud cry, not unworthy of a lion's roar when it kills its prey. Then suddenly he kneeled down on the deck, and folding his hands started to pray. This performance of his filled me with loathing for the man.

Aboard the Spanish prize the pirates, and those of its sailors who were able, were busy furling its sails. Rolling gently in the sea, the two ships lay less than a quarter-mile from each other The wind was from the west, warm and gentle. Isreal Hands had stopped praying. He looked at me, and grinning in true pirate fashion he said, "That was a good day's work, princeling."

Chapter 3

The end of the brigantine and an exhibition of skill

THE SPANISH SHIP WAS NAMED BONAVENTURA.
She was at least twice the length of the brigantine and broad-decked, carrying forty guns. This was a sturdy ship, yet not slow, three-masted and square-rigged with a large fore-and-aft sail on the mizzenmast. Even before capturing it, Captain Teach had decided that it would be his. Now that it was and we were on board, his crew was not large enough to man both the brigantine and the new vessel.

Giving not a thought to the gallant little ship that had served him so well, he decided to scuttle it. He always amazed me and frightened me by seeming not to care about anything. He could kill a man or not. The choice seemed of no importance to him.

I think the wounded among the Spaniards were killed by the pirates, for I saw none. The rest were given the choice of joining the pirates, or making for shore in the longboat of the brigantine. When none chose to join us, I thought of asking Blackbeard if I might be allowed to take my chance with the Spaniards in the longboat. But I decided against it, for I felt sure he would not allow it, and it would only make it more difficult for me to escape. From the very first moment that I stepped aboard the deck of the pirate ship, I had had only one thought: to escape. And each night before I slept I would plan yet another way to gain my freedom.

Captain Teach had a new name painted on the ship. She was now the *Queen Anne's Revenge*. A strange name for a pirate ship, I thought. What was Captain Teach revenging on behalf of Queen Anne, and who was she? Was she an English queen? I knew little of such things. Jamaica was so far away from that strange country that claimed to rule us. What was it like? Blackbeard told me that he was Bristol-born, as if that was something special. My mother once told me that she came from a city called York, and it was next to London, the most important city in the country. Bristol. York. They were merely sounds to me, not meaningful like Kingston, Spanish Town, or Port Royal.

"What say you, princeling? This is a ship, not an overgrown jollyboat masquarading as one." Captain Teach's hands caressed one of the cannons. "Forty cannons and all nine-pounders."

"Where will we be heading?" I asked. I had hoped that we would stay near Jamaica. I knew that my father would be only too willing to pay a ransom, for I was his only child.

"The Carolinas." Blackbeard smiled and looked over at the brigantine. Everything of value, even some of its sails and spars, had been taken aboard the *Queen Anne's Revenge*. "We shall blow it up, princeling", he announced. "Methinks the crew has grown thirsty from this day's work. It will be fitting to celebrate with a bit of fireworks. Mr. Morton, please!"

The ruffian who was in charge of the guns answered the call.

"Aye, what do you want? My throat is so dry I can hardly speak."

"Take another keg of powder and a slow fuse, and send that old ship to kingdom come. When you come back, you shall have as much to drink as you wish."

"A pity. She was a frisky one when the wind blew." The gunner looked at the brigantine.

"Aye, Mr. Morton. She served us well, and that is why I want to give her a proper burial. Take the jollyboat and be back before she blows up. There is wine on board here, and we can toast her in."

The gunner left and soon we saw the jollyboat on its way towards the brigantine. The breeze had died and neither ship moved. The captain ordered a cask of wine to be brought up on deck and spiked, but allowed no one to tap it before the jollyboat and its crew had returned. Our new ship had several pigs on board and some fowl as well. The largest of the pigs had been slaughtered, and was now being roasted in the galley. The delicious smell coming from that quarter reminded me how long it had been since we had last eaten.

"Now if this was a man-of-war, an English one, then I could keep the discipline, and if there was trouble I could have their backs combed with a cat-o'-nine-tails. But, princeling, we sail under the black flag, and a man turns pirate to be free, and he dreams of giving, rather than receiving the orders. So, since I see no clouds on the horizon and I do not smell a gale coming, I shall let the men drink until they have lost their senses. But stay away from them, for their knives will be loose in their sheaths. Pirates at the best of times have little sense, and when they are drunk they have none."

"Why did you turn pirate, Captain Teach?" We were both watching the jollyboat returning. "You are a very good sailor."

"Maybe just because of that, princeling." Blackbeard smiled. "I was too good a sailor for the forecastle, yet not considered good enough to tread the quarterdeck unless I touched my forelock first. Had I chosen my mother more wisely than I did, and known who my father was, I should never have chosen a profession like this one. Food for the gibbet, hangman's meat they call us. I tell you, princeling, if they hanged all who deserved it, few men would be left alive."

The jollyboat had come aside and the men had just climbed over the bulwark of the *Queen Anne's Revenge*.

"Is it ready?" Blackbeard shouted. The gunner nodded and yelled for wine.

Now all were given as much as their glasses, or cups could hold. Even I was given a glass by the Captain. Then everyone waited, staring at the brigantine that had been their home for more than a year.

When the explosion finally came, sending a burst of flame high up towards the mast-top of the unlucky vessel, Captain Teach drained his goblet and filled it up once more. It was a golden goblet and I wondered from whom he had stolen it.

I watched the brigantine, now engulfed in flames. Ships are man-made, yet they are strangely alive at the same time. It made me sad to see the end of something so beautiful.

"Get some food, princeling, and then go below and hide, for once my men have drunk enough, I shall not be captain until they are sober again." Blackbeard motioned for me to go where the cook was carving roasted pork. I was served a portion, and a very hard, stale biscuit as well. I retreated aft and hid myself behind the helm, where I ate my food. The pork was delicious, and the fat helped the dry biscuit to glide down. I still had half a glass of wine left, but I dared not ask for more.

The brigantine was still burning. The sun had set, but the horizon in the west was golden. Suddenly, there was another explosion from the smaller ship. Some ammunition must have been left in the powder magazine. I had heard Captain Teach giving orders for all the powder to be removed, and I recalled what he had said about pirates and the obeying of orders. I had disobeyed his order to hide below, because I did not want to go down into that hot and airless place.

The flames from the brigantine reflected in the water, making a double picture of the burning boat. Suddenly, it started heeling over, then righted itself again as if in pain, only to capsize completely. I could hear the sizzling as the water fought the fire and put it out. Then the ship disappeared and the night became doubly dark.

The pirates were singing, or maybe more correctly, screaming, for few of them had voices. But suddenly they grew silent as one strangely sweet voice rose above the others. I had never heard the voice or the song before, and I went from my hiding place to see who was singing.

From Jamaica sailed a ship,
High ho, and the winds do blow.
Its sails were white as fallen snow,
Its flag as black as hell below.
The wind blows free across the sea,
And brothers all we be.

The king wants to stretch our neck
And make us dance in the air.
But forty guns from our deck
Shall answer him so fair.
The wind blows free across the sea,
And brothers all we be.

A pirate is a high-born lad,
He owns the wide, wide ocean.
So let us be merry and not be sad
And thank the devil for our potion.
The wind blows free across the sea,
And brothers all we be.

Empty your cup, then fill it up.
Our lives are courage bound,
Our swords are sharp, our powder dry,
And the planks in the hull are sound.
The wind blows free across the sea,
And brothers all we be.

The singer was one of the youngest pirates. I did not think he had yet seen his twentieth summer. He was a handsome lad by the name of John Husk.

I had not heard the song before because he had just made it up. Suddenly someone shouted, "Boy, come here." I looked around not realizing that the "boy" was me. Then I saw the gunner, Mr. Morton, beckoning me. For a moment I thought of running down below, but being dragged back up on deck was so humiliating that instead I walked over to the man.

"Stand by the mast, boy." The gunner pushed me until I stood with my back against that giant spar. Then he measured ten paces and took his knife from his belt. Only then did I realize what his game was. All the pirates were looking at me and grinning in expectation. I looked for Captain Teach. He was there with a crooked smile on his face. I stared at the gunner, trusting he was not so drunk that he had lost his skill, and hoping that the fear I felt did not show on my face. The gunner raised his arm, and holding the point of the knife between two fingers, he threw it.

I heard the sound as the knife embedded itself in the wood, not an inch above my head. The feat was greeted with loud shouts of approval and cheers.

Blackbeard walked over and drew the knife from the mast. Laughing, he called for a candle. "Now, Mr. Morton, stand where you are and let me show you *my* skill. Light the candle and place it on Mr. Morton's head," he ordered. Taking one of his pistols from his belt, he loaded it with powder and bullet. So still was the air and so paralyzed the gunner, that the candle on his head was burning brightly, its flame straight up.

Very, very, slowly, Captain Teach's arm moved upwards, as all eyes watched the weapon in his hand. Then he shot, the sharp sound of the explosion echoing doubly loud in the stillness, and the candle's flame was extinguished. Again there were loud cheers as the gunner took the candle from his head and threw it overboard.

"Had you flinched, Mr. Morton, then I would have lowered my sight, and it would have been you, not the candle, that ended in the sea." Then turning to me, Blackbeard said, "Get below like I told you to, boy."

I ran quickly aft and down below to a berth that probably belonged to the servant of the Spanish captain. I lay awake for a long time, listening to the noises of the drunken pirates, scared that they would come below. No one did, and I finally fell asleep.

Chapter 4

John Husk and a skirmish with a man-of-war

IT WAS NEAR NOON. THE QUEEN ANNE'S REVENGE
was moving quickly through the waters, the wind was southeast, and we were on a western course.

"Did you make up the song that you sang last night?" I asked
the young pirate, John Husk.

"Aye," he smiled. "It was not much of a song, though I liked
the refrain."

"Are pirates truly brothers?" I asked. John was at the helm.
The ship was nearly deserted. Few of the pirates had left their
berths that morning. Captain Teach had been on deck, but had
not stayed long.

"They are brothers, all right, and like brothers, they hate each
other." John Husk grinned.

"Why?" I was surprised by his answer.

"Brothers are tied to each other. You cannot break the bond.
Your brother is your brother regardless of what kind of rogue
he is. Well, pirates are brothers in that same way. Once they

have sailed under the black flag, there is no escaping from that
family."

"Sir Henry Morgan did," I argued. "He became vice-governor
of Jamaica."

The young pirate nodded. "That is true, and yet I think he was
the worst of them. He would have sold his own mother if anyone
had cared to buy her. I like better his friend, Mr. Sharpe. Though
the king pardoned him as well, and made him a captain and gave
him a ship, he deserted King Charles' navy and sailed back here
under the black flag. I would have liked to have served under him."

"Better than Captain Teach?" I asked. John looked about him
before he answered.

"Blackbeard fears no one, not even himself. Courage he has, as
much as any man could want, but he is cruel. Be careful of him."

"He said last night that if Mr. Morton had flinched he would
have killed him. Do you think he would have?"

"You never know with him. You cannot trust him." Suddenly
he laughed. "Once, Captain Teach decided that he knew where
he would end up. So he had the hold sealed up and he, Mr. Morton, and Mr. Gibbens, sat there while they burned brimstone to
see which of them would last the longest in hell. The sulphur
smoke was thick, and they almost coughed their lungs out, but
Blackbeard stayed the longest."

"What was the most difficult, the throwing of the knife or
shooting out the flame of the candle?"

John Husk looked kindly at me. "I think the most difficult was
standing by the mast. You did well—all pirates admire courage."

"I was afraid," I admitted.

"Courage is the conquering of fear. A man who does not know
fear is more like a beast than a man. Yet a man who is ruled by fear
is neither man nor beast, he is nothing at all." The young pirate
turned to the lee side and spat, then repeated, "nothing at all."

"Captain Teach, he does not know fear?" I asked.

The pirate shrugged his shoulders. "Who knows who or what Blackbeard fears. Sometimes I think that's what he is searching for, is something to fear." John Husk looked up at the sails for a moment. They were well filled.

"Death," I said, for that seemed to me at that moment the greatest thing to fear.

But John laughed. "Death! No, that is nothing, and why fear nothing. Death is the final darkness of night, and that means sleep. I do not fear death and neither does Blackbeard. You know what I fear?" I shook my head. "I fear losing a leg or an arm. Have you ever seen the cripples lying outside the church showing stumps of their legs or arms to passersby hoping to obtain a coin through pity. That I fear, not death."

At that moment a cry sounded from the masthead, "Ship in the offing." John Husk smiled and ordered me to go below and wake Captain Teach.

The pirate was lying on the couch in the cabin that once had belonged to the Spanish captain. An attempt had been made to make the room elegant, and the couch itself had legs turned into the shapes of four golden dolphins. Now the place was a mess. Blackbeard was snoring with his mouth half-open, a sight more repulsive than frightening. I touched his shoulder and shook him gently. He opened one eye, recognized me, and closed it again. "There is a ship in the offing," I muttered.

"What kind?" Blackbeard grumbled and stretched himsef

"I don't know, sir. The helmsman sent me down to tell you."

"Run up and ask him." Blackbeard sniffed as if he smelled something unpleasant, which he very well might have for the cabin stank. "And ask its course, too."

I ran quickly to John Husk. He bellowed the questions to the man on watch in the masthead and the answer came ringing back.

"Methinks her a man-of-war, about our strength, and she has just changed course for us."

"Now you run and tell the captain. That ought to get the sleep out of his eyes." The young pirate grinned.

When I came back into the cabin, Blackbeard was asleep again. I touched his shoulder gently, and again he opened one eye. "What now, princeling?" he asked.

"She is a man-of-war and steering for us," I answered, eager to see Captain Teach's reaction to this news.

"A man-of-war, all eager for a bit of it. Why not? I thought I would sleep until dinner time, but all right, we will have a bit of war instead." Captain Teach sat up, yawned twice, and then rose. Two pistols were still in his belt, but he picked up a third one and stuck that into his belt as well.

In a short time all the pirates were on deck, some a little bleary-eyed and grumbling at having their sleep distrubed. But all worked under the orders of Mr. Morton in getting the guns ready and setting the topgallant sails as well as the royals. Captain Teach was busy watching the approaching ship through his telescope.

"In a fight like this, princeling, what is most important is speed and maneuverability, and you cannot have one without the other. Let me take the helm for a minute." Captain Teach was smiling with pleasure as he felt the movement of his ship through the great wheel under his hands. "She will do," he said, watching the gun being loaded and gotten ready. Then he handed the helm back to John Husk.

The approaching vessel was now near enough to be seen plainly. "Is she English, sir?" I asked.

"I have seen her before," John Husk said. "She is the *Scarborough*, of thirty guns operating out of Barbados."

"The *Scarborough*." Captain Teach tasted the name of his opponent. "We shall give her some scars, all right," he said, and issued further orders I did not understand.

"As soon as the broadside has been fired, take her about immediately under her stern. With a bit of luck, two of our guns shall rake her from there." By now the two ships were very near each other, and to my surprise I felt a pleasant, tense expectation. I looked at the captain and then at the young pirate at the helm. I could tell he felt it, too.

At the very moment when we were midship of each other our guns roared. The guns of the man-of-war answered, but just a little too late to cause serious damage. The *Queen Anne's Revenge* turned as the helmsman spun the wheel, and as we passed under the *Scarborough's* stern, two of our guns roared their cannonballs, ripping open her stern cabin. "That will air out the captain's cabin," Blackbeard said with a grin.

Queen Anne's Revenge was ready to engage the man-of-war again. But to our surprise, the *Scarborough* veered off and set a course for Barbados. "By God, she has had enough." Captain Teach laughed and then breathed deeply. The smell of burned powder still clung to the ship.

"At that moment when the dice are cast, just at the point of battle, a man feels more alive than at any other time in his life." Blackbeard looked at me, and then smiled almost kindly as he said, "I think you felt it."

I looked away, ashamed, for indeed I had "felt it."

Blackbeard ordered the helmsman to return to the old course, due westerly-northwest. Then, he went once more below, pausing just to give orders for the guns to be secured, and for powder and shot to be taken to the powder magazine.

Why had I felt so ashamed? Was it because of the moment of intimacy which had occurred between Blackbeard and me? I looked at the English warship that was fast disappearing. I had not tried to hide myself but had stood in plain sight for anyone to see and shoot at. I had felt no fear as the guns thundered. Shouldn't I have been frightened, I asked myself? But I found no answer. I had been no different from pirates. Again, shame engulfed me, but it was mixed with pride as well.

Chapter 5

Major Bonnet

"WE SHALL MAKE A PIRATE OF YOU YET," BLACK-beard grinned. "Yesterday you showed enough courage for the profession."

I shook my head. It still upset me that I had sided with the pirates during the skirmish with the man-of-war.

I wandered off to my favorite place on the ship by the bowsprit. The sound of the *Queen Anne's Revenge* cleaving the water was peaceful. The breeze blew from the southeast and our course was still towards the west. Out of the crest of a wave a school of flying fish took to the air, their scales glittering color-fully in the sunlight. A lone dolphin followed, staying close to the ship. If one could swim like that, I thought as I watched the dol-phin, I would swim right back to Jamaica. But then I laughed, for I would not be able to go ashore if I were a dolphin.

I spent all that morning thinking about my home, about Mary who had brought me up, and also about my father. He had hired tutors to teach me. Most of them had been beachcombers, loafers from England wrecked by cheap rum. They usually managed to stay sober while teaching me. They all claimed to have studied at Cambridge or Oxford Universities, and certain it was that now they were attending the school of hard knocks. My father had caught one arriving at our house drunk, and had thrown him from the veranda to the ground. I had felt sorry for the man, for he was the only one among my teachers whom I suspected was truly educated.

My father had declared on my tenth birthday that now I was a man, and that I should dine with him. The only trouble was that he was seldom at home. Most evenings I dined alone at a table so large that it could have comfortably seated sixteen. The servants would bring me food, but Mary, my playmate and my parents' slave, would serve.

As I sat in the bow of a pirate ship, I realized how strange my upbringing had been. "Princeling," I muttered. How apt was the nickname Captain Teach had given me, for surely I had been a little prince. "Princeling," I repeated with disgust and spat, not to the lee side but into the wind, and the spit flew back upon my clothes.

"Ship to port," the voice rang out from the masthead. I stood up, and shading my eyes, looked in that direction. It was a a small brigantine, fore and aft rigged on the mainmast, with a square sail on the slightly shorter foremast. Capain Teach gave orders for us to change course in order to intercept it. I wondered if it came from Jamaica, and if Blackbeard would let it sail once he had robbed it. If so, I might be able to send a message to my father.

Shots and powder were brought up and the guns were unfastened and loaded. A warning shot was fired and the black flag hoisted as we drew near to the much smaller ship. We expected it to surrender without a fight and were not surprised when it went into the wind and its crew started furling the sails. But it did come as a surprise, and caused much merriment, when the brigantine hauled up a flag as black as our own. As it turned, showing us its stern, I could read its name carved just beneath its taffrail, *Revenge Barbados*. I smiled, wondering what all these pirates were revenging. They seemed very fond of that word.

The brigantine had lowered its jollyboat. It was small and it seemed to carry no longboat. Two sailors rowed, and in the stern sat a portly gentleman. He was not young, and too fat to be very agile. With great difficulty he climbed up the companion ladder thrown down to him. He was very well dressed but not in a mar-itime fashion. His hair had once been blond, but was now mostly gray. He was clean shaven and not very tall.

He introduced himsef. "Major Bonnet, Captain of the *Revenge*."

"Captain Teach, master of the *Queen Anne's Revenge*. A tidy little craft you command. How many in your crew?"

"Forty eight, all stout men who fear nobody."

"And their captain is the stoutest of them all, I see. My men fear me, and that is the way I like them. Come below, captain, and drink a glass of wine, if it is not too early in the morning for you."

"I find it is seldom too early to drink, or for that matter, to eat." Major Bonnet glanced around at the pirates and for a moment his eyes met mine. He is a fool, I thought. Our captain is making fun of him.

On Blackbeard's orders, I followed the two pirate chiefs below.

More than a glass of wine was drunk! Two bottles were emp-tied, the major drinking the better part of them. As the wine went down, what little sense he had left him. They agreed to cruise together, with Captain Teach in command of the little pirate fleet.

"To a successful venture, Major." Captain Teach raised his glass and touched Bonnet's. "I will send you a man to help you, the best of my crew. Richard Stiles, he is called."

"My own men suit me. I do not want any strangers on board." The major put his empty glass down.

"Only the best is good enough for a companion-in-arms."
Blackbeard rose. "I shall miss Richard, but you shall have him,
and he won't be a stranger to you for long."

The major did not rise, but looking at me as if he had not
noticed me before, asked, "Is that boy your son?"

"Almost." Captain Teach sat down again. "I am thinking of
adopting him. "But in truth his father owns half of Jamaica. I
can't recall his name but it is on my glass. Princeling, what is your
father's name?"

"Jonathan Bernard," I answered, wondering if it was true that
he could not remember my father's name, or if it was done to
humiliate me.

"I have heard of him, I even think I sold your father some
slaves once." The major nodded thoughtfully. "I had a plantation
in Barbados myself, but not as large as your father's. Are you his
only son?"

"Yes, I am his only son."

"You mean your mother's only son. I am sure your father has
at least a dozen, but hardly as fairskinned as you." The major
broke out into a loud, unpleasant cackle.

The thought that I might have half-brothers and sisters all
over Jamaica was totally new to me. Yet I suspected that it
might be true. I looked at Blackbeard. He smiled not unkindly
at me.

"He has never thought of that," Major Bonnet laughed, as nas-
tily as before.

"The princeling knows little of life, he is an innocent babe.
Fetch us another bottle."

As I went to the pantry to get the wine, I remembered something that had happened once. My father had had a friend staying for dinner. On being asked if his wife was unwell, my father
had answered that his wife was permanently ill and never left
her room. His friend had shaken his head sadly. For the first time

I realized that my mother was mad. What Captain Teach had said was true—I was an innocent one, or had been one.

When I returned with the bottle, Captain Bonnet was blub-bering about his own son. "I have called him Samuel after my father. He is aboard the *Revenge*. His mother is dead. My wife killed her. It was a pity. I had bought Samuel's mother honest and fair." Major Bonnet's eyes filled with tears. "She was a good woman, even if she was brown, and she loved me."

On this last declaration, Major Bonnet staggered to his feet and demanded to be returned to his ship as he was feeling unwell.

With the help of Richard Stiles he managed to climb down to his jollyboat. Blackbeard and I watched, the pirate grinning as the major collapsed on the seat aft, almost capsizing the little craft.

"A fine captain he is, who can't hold his liquor," Captain Teach said and shook his head contemptuously. "We shall have our bit of sport with him." This last was said to Gibbens, who had been watching as well.

Chapter 6

Samuel

A WEEK OF LIGHT AND SHIFTING WINDS FOL-
lowed our meeting with Major Bonnet's *Revenge*. Once or twice
we saw a ship in the offing, that far, distant part of the sea just
visible from a ship, but night fell before we could reach them, and
when morning came, they were gone. On such still days the heat
became almost unbearable, and if we did not soon see land, we
would be running short of water.

Captain Teach got the idea of inviting the major on board the
Queen Anne's Revenge. The "invitation" was in fact a command
only lightly wrapped in politeness. I think he did it more out of
boredom than anything else.

"My dear Major, you are most welcome aboard my ship."
Blackbeard bowed with exaggerated courtesy as Major Bonnet
climbed over the bulwark.

"That rascal you sent me has taken command of my ship,"
spluttered Bonnet, not bothering to acknowledge the greeting.

"Richard is a grand sailor, though sometimes a little rough. He was brought up in the gutter and it shows. But the *Revenge* is still yours. He is merely to take charge of it while you are my guest."

"Am I a guest, or prisoner?" demanded the major.

"My most honored guest and brother-in-arms," Blackbeard replied affably. "Is that your servant?" he asked, pointing to a boy's grinning face just appearing on deck.

Major Bonnet looked sourly at the boy who was carrying a large portmanteau stuffed with the major's clothes. "He is a stupid boy," he said and looked away.

"Let me show you your cabin and let us have a drink to seal our friendship." Blackbeard put his hand lightly on the major's shoulder. He shook it off but still followed the pirate aft. As soon as the two captains had turned their backs, the "stupid boy" stuck out his tongue at them. Noticing me, he smiled as he followed them.

I had been watching the incident while standing near the mizzenmast, and now I retired to my favorite place in the bow of the ship. Stretching my legs out and resting my back against the part of the bowsprit that was inboard, I daydreamed about escaping from the pirate ship. We could not be far north of the Bahamas, I thought, and what wind there was, and current too, was carrying us south. If we got near one of the islands, I would try and swim for it.

A voice interrupted my thoughts. It was the boy who had carried the major's bag on board.

"I am Major Bonnet's slave and my name is Sam."

"Welcome onboard the *Queen Anne's Revenge*." I sprang to my feet, doffing an imaginary hat.

"Are you Captain Blackbeard's slave?" The boy asked as he seated himself. Denying vehemently that I was a slave, I threw myself down beside him.

"Are you his servant then? Does he pay you?"

"I don't get paid," I admitted, "but I am not his servant either."

"Do you obey him?" he persisted and I nodded. "Then you are his slave." Sam declared, grinning. Noticing that this upset me, he added, "Most people are slaves, they just don't know it. That is the difference between them and me. Do you think they are free?" A wave of his hand took in all the pirates on board. "They think they are free but they are not, and they will all end up dancing in the air."

"And what will happen to your master, Major Bonnet. Will he end up dangling from the gallows, too?" I asked.

"He deserves no better. Look." Sam lifted his shirt and showed me his back, criss-crossed with the lash marks from a whip.

"Did he do that?" Some of the stripes looked old, but others were still red welts.

"I keep a score of the beatings, and if and when the time is right, I shall pay him back. When he is drunk, he either gets mean or sad. When he is mean he beats me. When he is sad he cries and tells me that he is my father."

"Do you think he is?" I asked, recalling what I had heard in the captain's cabin.

"My mother said he was, and she had no reason to lie. The major's wife—and she is a tartar—had my mother beaten less than an inch of her life, so I think it is true enough."

"What is your mother like?" I asked, trying very unsuccessfully to conjure up a picture of my own. "Is she beautiful?"

Sam sighed. "I have been told that she was. But a slave's good looks don't last, especially not in the sugarcane field. She was sent there when I was born, and when she died two years ago she was an old crone. She claimed that I had brought her bad luck, as if a slave ever could have good luck. Her bad luck was not me, or the major, but his wife. She saw to it that my mother got the heaviest work, even in the cane field. She is meaner than the devil's grandmother. She beat the slaves and servants for the joy of it, and I am not sure that she did not beat the major as well. I think he turned pirate to get away from her."

"What does she look like?" I asked, expecting to be told that she was as ugly on the outside as she was on the inside.

"She is handsome enough, younger than the major." Sam yawned and stretched himself. "She never mistreated me. I think she liked me. But she would have made a better pirate captain than my father." The thought made him laugh. "But I would pity the poor sailors who fell into her clutches if she was in command."

"Sail in the offing," a voice called from the crosstrees. I looked up to see John Husk on watch.

Shading my eyes I tried to spot the ship myself. It was only a sloop, its sail but not its hull visible just above the horizon.

Through half-closed eyes Sam looked at me. "What is it?" he asked.

"An island sloop not worth changing course for." I looked at my friend for I already thought of Sam as such. His skin was brown and his hair straight, and yes, I thought, Major Bonnet could very well be his father.

"A pity it is not an English frigate," Sam closed his eyes.

"If an English frigate sank us, we might drown as well, have you thought of that?" I said with a grin, noticing that the major and Blackbeard had both come on deck.

"True. Can you swim?" Sam opened his eyes again.

"Like a fish." I replied, Blackbeard was scrutinizing the sloop through his telescope.

"In that case you will drown, for fish swim where we can't breathe. I can swim like a dolphin. The major can't swim. I would love to see him drown, or better yet, the sharks eating him."

I heard Captain Teach give an order. We were changing course, going after the sloop. Major Bonnet's *Revenge* was a few cable lengths aft of us. "Have you not thought of escaping, of running away?"

"Barbados is not a large island. Slaves who run away are usually caught."

"In Jamaica, slaves who run away go to live in the mountains. We call them maroons."

"And are they never caught?" Sam opened his eyes wide and sat up.

"If they get up into the mountains they are never caught. The maroons are fierce fighters." As the *Queen Anne's Revenge* had changed its course, the sails no longer shaded us where we were sitting. I got up, and the hull of the sloop was now clearly visible.

"If I had lived on Jamaica, then I should have run away long ago." Sam stood up as well.

"If we could get a boat, big enough to be seaworthy but small enough that we could hanlde her, then we could sail for Jamaica." I looked at Sam to see if the idea pleased him.

"Get one? You mean steal one. That is not so easy. But if we can, then I am with you. I want to get to that island and become ... what was it you called them, the ones that live in the mountains?"

"Maroons," I grinned, and then held out my hand. Sam looked surprised at first, but then he grabbed it.

A gun was fired when we got near the little sloop, commanding it to heave-to so we could send someone on board. But its captain paid no attention to the shot, and kept her course. It was but a small island boat and would contain little of value to us. Now Blackbeard ordered four of our cannons to be loaded, two on either side. *Queen Anne's Revenge* went about and as it passed the smaller vessel to port, two guns were fired. One shot went through the sloop's main-sail, the other went wide. Again we went about, and now the guns on the starboard side were fired. This time our gunnery had improved, and the sloop's mast was cut in two.

The little craft went into the wind and its crew waved to us to signify that they had given up. I expected Blackbeard to heave-to, but he didn't. Our ship went about and passed the sloop once more, and again our guns fired. This time both charges went home, leaving the little boat a sinking wreck.

"That will teach him to obey a command given by me." Captain Teach laughed and ordered me to fetch glasses of rum for each member of the gun crews. I brought the drink, and pouring for our chief gunner, Philip Morton, asked, "Why did Captain Teach sink it?"

He shrugged his shoulders and drank his tot of rum in one gulp, and then demanded a second. I poured it, expecting the shrug to be my only answer when he said. "His name is Captain Teach and now those on board the sloop have been taught a lesson." Then he laughed at his own joke and swallowed his second tot.

Much later, when our masters had drunk themselves into a stupor, I asked Sam the question again—why did he sink that little boat? It was nearly midnight and the ship was deserted except for the sailors on watch. We were sitting in the stern, Sam watching our wake, which was luminous as if the sea was alight.

"Why do you care?" Sam looked up at me. "Does anyone know why a snake bites?"

"I understand why he turned pirate. He was poor and wanted to be rich, that makes sense. But why sink that boat? There were two children onboard, about our age."

"It is as if the stars of heaven have fallen into the sea." Sam looked up at me. "What matters to a slave is to escape the whip. He need not think of anything else." He turned back to stare at our luminous wake. "Look!" he exclaimed and pointed to a dolphin that was pursuing us in a rain of sparks.

"Maybe I haven't been a slave long enough," I said with a grin.

"Or whipped often enough," Sam laughed. "He did it to show off to the major, or maybe to himself. It doesn't matter a bit to us. We will steal a boat and sail to Jamaica. Where is it now? Ahead or astern?"

"Jamaica? In about that direction," I said, pointing southeast.

"Then we shall get there." Sam held out his hand and I grasped it, and we both laughed.

Chapter 7

The storm

CAPTAIN TEACH LOOKED OUT OVER THE SEA. IN the horizon to the east some dark clouds were gathering. "I do not like this swell. There is dirty weather somewhere near."

"The wind is light," the man at the wheel observed, which was true enough. But it made it difficult for the *Queen Anne's Revenge* to keep her course as she would slide sideways down the big, lazy waves.

"We shall have wind soon enough." Blackbeard ordered more sails to be furled. "I do not like its direction." The captain pointed towards the east. "We are too near the Bahama Bank. If we get blown there with sea like this..." Turning towards Major Bonnet he asked. "Can you swim?"

The major's face was white, and he was holding on to a stay. "No, but it doesn't matter. I think I will just as soon drown." Major Bonnet then leaned over the railing and offered up to the fishes of the sea whatever he had eaten that day.

"Go below and lie down." Blackbeard saw me standing

nearby and said, "Find the major's boy and tell him to come and help his master."

Sam was sitting on the deck near the main mast. I was sure that Blackbeard had seen him, but felt it was below his dignity to call the boy. Sam was not feeling too well, himself. "I hate the sea," he said as I delivered Blackbeard's command.

I looked out over the rolling waves that rose and fell with monotonous constancy.

"We are going to have a storm," I said. Sam nodded in agreement and staggered off to help his master. I watched them go below, the major leaning on Sam's shoulder, then I returned aft.

"You have good sea legs and I think an iron stomach, princeling. Would you dare to climb the masts now?" Blackbeard grinned.

I looked up at the huge spars that swung wildly in great arches against the sky as the *Queen Anne's Revenge* rolled in in the turbulent waves. "No, I would not care to," I admitted.

"Princeling, that was well said. Only a fool would boast of wanting to. Look!" Blackbeard pointed to the east. The black clouds had risen and now covered most of the sky in that direction, but it was the sea the pirate was pointing to. The black waves had suddenly dressed themselves in white in the eastern horizon. A gentle warm breeze from the south now suddenly changed into a storm from the east.

The sails filled and the ship heeled over as the wind hit us. All we carried was the mainsail and the smallest of staysails, and the mainsail ripped in two and then into tatters. "Let her run with the wind," Captain Teach ordered, and pushing aside the man at the wheel, took command of it himself. "We have no choice but to obey, princeling. It was better to lose a sail than a mast. She will weather the storm just so long as we keep her away from the bank." Captain Teach was grinning and I thought he was enjoying it.

"How far away are we?" I screamed, for the noise of the sea and the wind tearing at the tattered sails was overpowering.

"Far enough I hope, princeling, to weather to the north of the bank. If not..." the pirate shrugged his shoulders. At that moment the sea broke as it hit us. Part of it engulfed the aft deck sending me sprawling against the bulwark. Lying there, drenching wet, while the water drained out through the scuppers, I looked up at Captain Teach. His mouth was moving, but I could not hear what he was saying. Suddenly I realized he was singing.

"We were nearly in as great a danger as I have ever been, but the rudder held." Blackbeard looked at me as I staggered to my feet again. "You are all wet. Go below." At that moment the little staysail burst. "The wind on the mast, well, why not." The pirate laughed and then ordered me once more to go below.

Below deck the noise of the storm became muted, but the clash of the waves against the hull made up for it. As I walked by Major Bonnet's cabin I looked in. The major was lying in his bunk moaning, vomit all over his clothes. He was a pitiful sight. Sam was sitting on the end of bunk, not in much better condition. Seeing me, Major Bonnet made an effort to sit up, and pointing to Sam he declared, "He is my son, my only child." Then he sank back on the pillow. I looked at Sam, who made an effort to smile. "I am an evil man," the major groaned. "God have mercy upon me. You are a good boy and your father a fine man...oh, why did I ever turn pirate." To my surprise, I saw tears running down the major's cheeks. "It is my bad luck, it follows me...it is my fate."

At that moment the *Queen Anne's Revenge* keeled over, sending everything that was not tied down flying. Then she righted herself again, but only just. I wondered if we had been near-pooped again and if Captain Teach was all right. The major had folded his hands and was saying the Lord's Prayer over and over again. I smiled at Sam, and then went to my own bunk. If I was going to drown I might as well get some rest first.

I fell readily asleep, and when I woke a few hours later, I could feel by the movement of the ship that the worst of the storm was over. My clothes were still wet, but I got dressed and went on deck. A few sails had been set, and the *Queen Anne's Revenge* was on a northerly course. The sea was still very rough, and she was lurching in the waves. I held on to a stay while looking about. The sky had cleared and the sun was out, but low in the horizon, and a few white clouds were scurrying across the blueness.

Whitecaps were everywhere, but not far distant to the west rose a menacing surf. I could see a low island as well, and I thought that must be the Bahama Bank with its myriad of little islands. Captain Teach was no longer at the wheel but standing at the bulwark, contemplating the sight.

"Is that the bank?" I asked, knowing full well that it was.

"Aye, and a little too near for comfort." Captain Teach shook his head.

"But we are heading north," I said, surprised, for I could see no danger in the surf that was plainly to the west of us.

"Princeling, our bow is pointing north and we are heading that way, but we are moving west as well. The current, waves, and wind are taking us there. But I think we will weather it," Blackbeard grinned. "That was a great blow. Twice I thought we were done for, but she righted herself. She is a good one, maybe not as fast as some, but sturdy. Were you scared, princeling? Did you pray to your maker?"

"No, but Major Bonnet did. Just after I went below, when a great wave must have hit us. I heard him. He had been very sick."

Captain Teach grinned. "That was the second time we were near getting pooped, and I almost lost my hold on the wheel. That wave rose in back of us like a mountain and then suddenly it broke, and instead of lifting us it came tumbling down upon us."

"Where is the *Revenge*?" I asked. Maybe because we had been talking about the major I suddenly remembered his ship. Black-beard pointed aft.

The *Revenge* was a few miles astern, but a good deal northeast as well, so it would have no trouble weathering the bank.

"A storm like that is better preacher than most ministers." Captain Teach put his telescope to his eye and looked towards the island to the west. "They say the gallows, too, are great for conversion," he mumbled, and then satisfied with what he had seen he handed the telescope to me.

"Put it back in the cabin, princeling, we are in no danger now. If you see the major, tell him that he no longer need fear drowning, only the noose."

I did not give the major Blackbeard's message, for he was soundly asleep. But I told it to Sam whom I found sitting on my bunk.

"It was very near, wasn't it?" he asked.

"As near as you can get without getting there. Were you afraid?"

"I think I was too sick to be afraid. There were moments when I wished more for death than to escape it. The cabin stinks, and so does the major. He is sleeping in his vomit like a pig in its sty."

"Come on up above, you will feel better there. I saw an island to the west of us." I paused by the ladder. "You know, it is strange how being near death makes you feel so very alive."

Chapter 8

The race

"WHAT DOES IT MEAN THAT WE WERE ALMOST pooped?" Sam asked. We were sitting up by the bowsprit. The sea had calmed and the storm was only a memory now.

I repeated what John Husk had told me, for I had asked him the very same question. "When you are running for it, that is, with the wind and waves behind you, especially if you have no sails up like we did, then your speed and the wave's are almost the same. Now the running sea behind you can build up in a giant wave. When it catches up with you it does not lift your ship, but breaks over it. Then if the rudder does not hold you on your course, your ship could turn sideways to the wave and then…" I crossed my neck with the flat of my hand, repeating not only the sailor's words, but imitating the motion he had made when he had finished instructing me.

"I think I prefer dying on land rather than in the sea, though it looks pretty enough now." Sam grinned. "I don't know why, but the idea of the fishes eating me is unpleasant."

"You prefer the worms?" I asked, thinking that I might turn sailor, though I did not imagine myself climbing the mast, but as a captain of a ship ordering others to do it.

"Not much of a choice." Sam stretched himself. "Now that the sun is shining and the sea is calm, the major no longer claims me as his son. He cursed me soundly this morning for not getting his clothes as clean as he would like them. They were so filthy that I scrubbed them with a brush for an hour."

"He is a strange man, your father." Above me several gulls were circling.

"No he is not, not really. He is a weak man, but he taught me to read and write. When I am his son he can be kind, but then suddenly it is as if he becomes aware of the color of my skin. Then I become not only a slave but also a reminder of what he is. I would have been sold long ago, or been worked to death in the cane field...do you know whom I am named after?"

"No," I shook my head, though I did in fact remember the major telling Captain Teach that night in the cabin.

"His father's name was Samuel Bonnet. According to the major, he was at least a general. But I think that is a rank the major has awarded him, not the king." Sam smiled, then suddenly grew serious. "He is a foolish man who shall probably end up dangling from a rope. You are right. We must escape before they are caught, or we may end up keeping them company."

The water had changed color and was growing shallower, and now there were more birds. "We are getting near land. I saw a pelican not long ago, and they do not fly far from shore. We have passed north of the Bahamas and keeping a westerly course. We must be near the Carolinas."

"The Carolinas." Sam wrinkled his brow. "They belong to the king?"

"Oh, yes. My father once had business there, in Charles Town and it is very rich, so my father says."

"Your father, too, is very rich, so he should know." Sam grinned. "The major said that I should make friends with you."

"Is that why you did it?" I was surprised, for though it was true that my father was wealthy, I had lived so alone in our big house, that I did not yet know that the rich are never short of friends.

"Oh, yes, I always obey my master," Sam laughed. "Besides, it was easy. I liked you."

"Did he want you to spy on me?" I asked.

"Major Bonnet never knows what he wants. Your father is rich, and the major licks the boots of anyone who is rich or powerful. Since he could not lick your father's boots, he ordered me to lick yours."

I looked down at my bare feet, then lifted my leg and stretched it in Sam's direction. He sniffed and declared that I would have to wash it first before he did any licking, and at this we both burst out laughing.

"Blackbeard is powerful, at least on the *Queen Anne's Revenge*, but I can tell the major does not like him," I said.

"He hates him. He told me that he hoped he lived long enough to see Captain Teach hanged."

"Blackbeard won't ever be hanged," I said, feeling sure that this was true. "He will die fighting."

"You may be right. But the major will, I can tell you. And if he is caught and condemned to be hanged, he will cry all the way to the gibbet."

"And would you like to see him hanged?" I asked. "Just like the major would like to see Captain Teach dangle from the crosstree?"

Sam got up, looked out over the sea, and then sat down again. "I don't know. I could kill him ... yes, that I could, if for no other reason than for the stripes on my back. But that is a private matter between him and me. No, I should not like to see him hanged. He is my father."

I realized that my question had not been kind, and I leaned over and touched his shoulder. Sam smiled and I said, "I am glad the major ordered you to become my friend and that you obeyed."

We sat for a while saying nothing, half-asleep in the warm sunshine, listening to the sound of the ship's bow crushing the little waves, as it forged ahead. Then suddenly a voice bellowed from the crosstree. "Ship to windward." We both jumped up, and true enough, ahead of us was a vessel keeping almost the same course as ours. Since the wind was light we carried all the sails we could muster. We would have to catch up with it before night, for in the darkness we would be sure to lose it.

It was a long race. Blackbeard had a spritsail rigged, and maybe that made the difference. About an hour before sunset we were within hailing distance, but sailing in the same direction, we could not aim our guns at it.

"Princeling, I think its captain has gold in his purse." Captain Teach grinned as he ordered the guns on the starboard side unlashed and loaded. "We shall relieve him of its weight." A pirate was hauling up the black flag. It had a skeleton devil holding an arrow in his right hand and an hour glass in his left. The arrow pointed to a heart. What it all meant I think only Blackbeard knew.

"Heave to, if you don't want a broadside," Captain Teach bellowed. An answer came in the form of a bullet that whistled close to his head. The pirate grinned as if that reply had been to his liking. Some small-arms firing now began between the two ships. One pirate was wounded but it was a mere scratch. Slowly we were catching up, but as our prey was windward of us as we caught up, she stole our wind and we could not overtake her. Captain Teach now gave orders for the guns on the port side to be made ready. Taking the wheel himself, he changed course in order to pass the other ship to windward. But its captain was no fool, and changed course, too, trying to keep us on his lee side.

"I like him, princeling." Blackbeard nodded to emphasize his words. "He is a sailor, not a clodhopper that has taken to the sea." I grinned, but stopped as a bullet grazed my shoulder, tearing my jacket.

"A near-miss." Blackbeard laughed.

The sun was setting, huge and golden on the horizon, and still we had not managed to loosen one cannon shot at our prey. "Princeling, we will board her," Captain Teach grinned. "If the crew is as brave as its captain, it will be a fight worth recalling. The pirate shouted some orders I did not understand, but the crew understood and found to their liking.

Some of the pirates stuck the blades of their knives between their teeth, giving them a ferocious appearance. Others were getting ready some long ropes with iron hooks on their ends. Seeing my confused look, Blackbeard said, "Grappling irons...we throw them across to tie the ships together."

Slowly, almost inch by inch, we crept near our victim. The pirates ducked beneath the bulwark to escape the small-arms fire from our opponent. Blackbeard did not hide, and when we were but a few yards away, he let Gibbens take the wheel. A pirate gave him two lighted, slow-burning matches which he stuck in his long hair; across his back he slung a bandoleer containing three pistols; and taking the sword handed him, he ran forward to join his crew ready to board.

Fascinated, I watched it. Now we were so near that we could see the expressions on the faces of the crew on the other ship. Our bowsprit was level with their stern, then the foremast, and a moment later the grappeling hooks were cast and the two ships were tied together. The race was over, now came the fight, the slaughter.

Chapter 9

The slaughter

THE TWO SHIPS WERE NOW SECURELY TIED together, their spars and rigging bashing against each other. No one was at the helm of either ship, and the wheels turned as the waves and current played with their rudders. Gibbet had abandoned his post as soon as he had seen Blackbeard entering the other ship. Drawing his cutlass, he had jumped the bulwark as agile as a cat.

From where I stood I had a perfect view of the deck of our prey. She flew the flag of Spain, and I guessed that she had been on her way to Cuba. Most of the pirates on the *Queen Anne's Revenge* had served on privateers during the war against Spain, and I had often heard them talk with venom of their foes from those times. They had little love for Spaniards, and whenever a ship flying that flag fell into their clutches, they treated its crew cruelly and without mercy. The Spaniards knew this and fought fearlessly, none of them begging for quarter, knowing that there was little chance of it being given them.

The Spanish captain was a true hero. He was young, and I thought him handsome. Blackbeard had sought him out immediately and the two men were fighting a duel to death. Blood was flowing from Captain Teach's arm, but it was only a scratch which I was later ordered to bandage.

Blackbeard was the better swordsman and forced his opponent to retreat further aft. I could see the expressions on their faces. The Spaniard's was one of sternness, whereas Blackbeard's was disfigured by a grin worthy of his master, the devil.

They danced around the helm of the Spanish ship, Blackbeard lunging with his sword and the young man skillfully warding off each thrust with his. On the third round the Spaniard's foot caught in a rope lying on the deck and he stumbled. That ended the fight. Blackbeard cut his opponent's right arm and sent his sword flying. The Spaniard looked at the blood spurting from his arm. An artery had been cut.

Then in a few strides, he was at the bulwark of his ship and, using his left arm, he swung himself over the side and into the sea. Blackbeard went to the railing and peered into the waters, and I did the same. I could see nothing, then the fin of a big shark cut through the water, and I looked away.

I had seen neither Major Bonnet nor Sam during the fight. Now suddenly they both appeared. The major was dressed in what I thought was some kind of military uniform, a bright, swallowtailed coat laced with gold. His sword was drawn, and with great difficulty he climbed the bulwark of our ship and onto the Spanish one. One of his coattails got caught between the two ships' sides and tore as he jumped. His misadventure seemed to surprise him. He took off what was left of his coat, called for Sam and handed it to him. Now he was ready to enter the fray once more. Luckily for him, none of the Spaniards still fighting noticed him, for if they had, he would surely have been killed. He looked around as if searching for an opponent worthy of his mettle. Then, he suddenly burst into action, thrusting his sword into the chest of a wounded Spaniard lying on the deck.

"My father is a very brave man." Sam, carrying what was left of the major's coat, had joined me. "Since there were no women or children to fight, he had to be satisfied with a dying man." Sam shook his head in wonder.

"The Spanish captain is dead. Captain Teach wounded him, and when he saw that all was lost, he jumped into the sea." I described the brave fight he had fought, and how I had afterwards seen the fin of a shark break the surface of the water.

"There will be lots of food for them." Sam was looking at the deck of our prize. It was covered in blood and gore. The pirates had killed all of the Spaniards, but quite a few of their comrades were dead as well.

"A good day's work," I said sarcastically, recalling the words that I heard Isreal Hands say once.

"Which is more than can be said for my father," said Sam. "On the whole, I think I prefer being his slave to being his son. Where is Blackbeard?"

"I think he went below to search the ship. Now that the murdering is over the stealing can begin." The deck of the Spanish ship was almost deserted, and like hungry rats the pirates were scurrying to ransack their prize. Suddenly, I noticed a thin spiral of smoke emerging from the canvas covering of a hatch. "She is on fire!" I exclaimed, pointing to the smoke.

"And we are tied to her above as well as below." Sam looked up at the masts. Our rigging and the Spaniard's were entangled and the two ships would not be easily freed from each other.

The smoke became black and heavier. Then suddenly an explosion in the Spanish ship's hold blew off the hatchcover sending up clouds of smoke. As we were to leeward of the vessel the smoke blew over us. Now all the pirates returned, some of them carrying whatever they had found worth picking up. Shouting orders, Captain Teach slung a leather bag at me to take below to his cabin. I waited a moment to watch Major Bonnet, who was astride the two shipsides. The ships parted and I thought for sure the major would fall into the sea. But a pirate grabbed one of his legs and in a most undignified fashion hauled him aboard the *Queen Anne's Revenge*.

Even below I could smell the smoke, and I hurriedly threw the leather bag on Blackbeard's bunk. It was full of coins—I could feel them through the leather.

I returned on deck. Smoke and flames poured from the other ship. Most of the pirates were aloft, untangling the rigging and cutting it when necessary. Blackbeard was pointing and shout-ing orders, while other pirates had grabbed loose spars to pry us away from the burning ship. But it was as if the Spaniard would not let go of its embrace.

How soon before the fire would reach its rigging and then ours? It would have been a just revenge, but at the very moment when flames reached the mainsail of the Spanish boat, the *Queen Anne's Revenge* was freed. Ever so slowly, the two ships parted in the light breeze and we sailed out of the cloud of smoke that engulfed our prey.

"I wonder who did it?" Sam said. I shrugged my shoulders for how could I know. But at that very moment the question may have been answered.

On the smoke-free aft of the Spanish ship appeared a woman with a child—a boy, I think, about ten years of age. She stood watching our ship intently while her own was burning. Then she raised her hand over her head gesturing in our direction.

"That is a brave one," Captain Teach said at the helm, lifting his hand in a mock salute. "She almost took us with her." Then he set the course northwest and gave the wheel to one of the pirates. My eyes were glued to the burning ship and all its flaming sails. There was another explosion, and this time she must have been hulled for very shortly after she sank.

"Come below, princeling," Captain Teach ordered. As soon as we were in his cabin, he stripped of his coat and shirt. A gash on his right arm was still bleeding. He took a bottle of brandy and poured some onto the wound. Then, giving me some bandages cut from an old shirt, he ordered me to bind it. I obeyed, and saw the wound was not deep.

"A brave man and a brave wife. They would have been worthy to have in the brotherhood, better than some." Captain Teach spat, probably thinking of Major Bonnet. Then he slung himself into his berth and indicated that I could go. I left, noticing that his hand was fondling the leather purse.

Chapter 10

John Husk's life story.

MY LOVE IS FAR AWAY,
Upon the foaming sea.
Home I must stay,
Lonely though I be
'Til he comes back to me.

My father does scold,
He wants me to wed
A farmer ugly and old.
But I will have none instead
Of my sailor boy so bold.

My father can curse,
My mother can weep
For the loss of a golden purse.
But I my promise will keep
'Til he comes back to me.

It did not matter what John Husk sang. Some of his songs were crude, but the sweetness of his voice would nearly always cause my eyes to grow moist. Of all the pirates, he was the only one I liked. He not only treated me kindly but Sam as well. That was rare, for most of the pirates had little use for anyone whose skin was not as white as theirs. We were sitting in the bow, John Husk on a coiled rope and in his hand his lute.

"Did she marry the sailor or the farmer?" I asked smiling.

"The farmer, naturally. She had some good sense as did her father and mother."

"But in your song she promises to be true," I objected surprised.

"A song is but a dream, a song is nothing." The pirate struck the strings of his instrument. "No one waits for the sailor boy except the sharks in the ocean."

His hands moved nimbly and he began to sing again.

> Jack Tar is a sprightly boy,
> He loves the girls but leaves them.
> Play with your dolls and your toys
> For I am off to sail the seas
> And I must leave you

He stopped, a frown on his face, and looked up at the masts and sky. "There was more to that but I can't recall it." Then suddenly he smiled. "It is one I made up a long time ago. It doesn't matter."

"You do not write them down?" I asked.

"That is a skill I never learned." John Husk frowned. "I keep them all in my head, those I make up myself as well as those I hear others sing." Again his fingers played with the strings of his instrument. "There are so many songs in my head that it is no wonder if some of them should fall out when I shake it." This idea pleased John Husk so much that he laughingly shook his head, and I almost expected to see several verses fall out of it.

"I wish I could sing," Sam observed, "but I can't. The people in the cane fields are always singing. If they couldn't sing, I think their fate would be even harder to bear."

"Did your mother sing?" I asked. Sam nodded but said nothing.

"I have neither a father nor a mother," John Husk grumbled.

"Everyone's got a father and a mother," I objected.

"Everyone but me." The pirate looked at me and frowned. "I may have been dropped from heaven. I was found on the steps of a church in Bristol. The vicar there gave me the name of John, and from Mother Husk who took me in for a price, comes my other name. She claimed that I had not dropped from heaven, but popped up from another place below." John Husk laughed. "She was a thrifty lady. A shilling a month was what they paid her, and for that she bought clothes and fed me. True the clothes were but rags, and as for the food, the rats in the harbour ate better than me. Her voice was cracked from the gin she drank, but sing she could." The pirate paused for a moment. "I was but five years old—nay, maybe only three—when she started me singing in every ale house in town, and she drank up every cobber I earned. But bless her, she taught me a lot of songs."

"Did she teach you to play the lute as well?" I asked.

"Such an instrument for a beggar boy." The pirate shook his head at my stupidity. "That I learned much later." With pride, he looked down at the lute he cradled in his arms like a much-loved infant. "I once had a little tin flute. The vicar who gave me the name John, and he had a right to give that to me for it was his own, bought me the tin whistle in the market one day. I think that was the happiest day in my life. I played all night until Mother Husk took it away from me, saying the noise made her head ache."

"Did she give it back to you?" Sam asked.

"She did. She was not a bad old cow, though she had her tempers and could be mean. She died one winter night, when I was ten or so. Fell in the street coming home from wherever she had been drinking the gin. She didn't get up and it was cold. After that, I took to playing my flute in the marketplace and singing in

the taverns as before. And all the cobbers I earned were mine."
He laughed and we laughed, too.

"But how did you get to be a sailor?" Sam demanded.

"It happened the summer after old Mother Husk had died. I
was playing and singing in an inn called The Sailor's Rest, when
a group of tars there decided they liked my skill. They gave me
something to drink and a shilling, not the king's but their own. I
was asleep when the place closed and when I woke up it was
dawn and I was aboard their ship." John Husk stopped and picking up his lute began to sing.

> It was down the river and out to sea,
> And never again my mother I will see.
> High ho, the wind blows fresh and free
> A sailor's life and lot for me.
> So scrub the deck and climb the mast,
> And work as long as your life will last.
> High ho, the wind blows fresh and free
> A sailor's life and lot for me.

Just as the pirate sang the last line, a voice from the crosstrees
sang out. "Land ahead." We all rushed to the bulwark to look,
and there it was—a long low line on the horizon. America. The
Carolinas.

Chapter 11

I become Blackbeard's ambassador

IN THE BATTLE WITH THE SPANISH SHIP, SEVERAL
of the pirates had been wounded. Sam and I had been told to help
the carpenter in nursing them. Two had died the day after the
battle, and they had been dispatched to Davy Jone's locker, sewn
up in their hammocks with a couple of shots added for weight.
Now, Owen Roberts may not have been much of a doctor, but
both as a surgeon and carpenter he had some claim to fame, for
one of the pirates aboard *Queen Anne's Revenge* had a wooden
leg. The carpenter had not only cut off his leg, but also fashioned
his wooden one. The pirate was uncommonly proud of it. It had
been carved from mahogany into the shape of a dolphin.

"The only medicine I have left is for those who suffer from a
loose stomach, and that is not good for wound fever." Owen
Roberts shook his head and looked at his six patients lying in
their hammocks on the upper forecastle deck. "I must get some
more medicine, princeling."

"How are you going to do that?" I asked, for though we were

cruising within sight of the shore of the Carolinas, I could see no way of us getting it.

"I shall tell Captain Teach that I need it. To get it is not a carpenter's job but a captain's." With those words he left us.

"Do you think he knows anything about doctoring?" I asked Sam, who was pulling a rope attached to an enormous fan which did circulate the air a little. This was a contraption that the carpenter had made. I had never seen one before.

"I don't know." Sam nodded in the direction of the pirate nearest him. "I think this fellow has been dead since sunrise."

I went over to look. The pirate's head was bandaged but his head wound was only a scratch. It was the bullet he had received in his stomach that was serious. His open eyes stared up at me, seeing nothing. I waved my hand in front of them—he was dead alright. The night before he had begged for water, but the carpenter had not given him any. Now he was going to get water enough, a whole ocean full of it.

"Boy!" One of the patients with a leg wound called me. I went and stood beside his hammock. "Do you believe in God?" he asked.

"Yes," I mumbled, wondering at the same time if I really did, or if anyone did. Most of the pirates proclaimed belief, but if that was the truth, how could they do the gruesome acts I had seen them do.

"Hell. Yes, I believe in hell. But as for the other place, no!" The pirate smiled. "If such a place exists then God lives a lonely life, for I have known of no one who deserved to go there. I am a beast, but so are all men, and women, too. Why are we like that, boy? Tell me that!"

"I don't know," I said and shook my head. But then remembering the story of the fall of man I added, "It was because we ate the apple."

The pirate grinned. "That's an old tale. I have often thought about it. When I was a youngster like you, I was a God-fearing lad who attended Sunday school. I remember once asking the vicar if Adam ate the whole apple or just took a bite. The vicar called me a silly boy, but what I asked was not so stupid. I think he only ate a bite, and that is why we still don't know the difference between good and evil. Now if he had eaten it all, or picked himself a bushel of them, then hell would be empty today."

I could not help smiling at the idea. It was something I had never thought of. "Did Eve take a bite from the apple as well?" I asked.

"Aye, Adam took one, but she took two. Do you want to hear the proof of it? The pirate risks his life and his limbs on the sea, living a life a dog would not care for. Then when he comes ashore with his pockets full of doubloons, how long do they stay there? Why, before a week is over every one of those golden coins have ended up in a woman's purse. That is proof that Eve took two bites at least, if not three, and poor Adam only one."

I agreed, for it was true that pirates spent their money recklessly, maybe because they sensed in a way that it had never been truly theirs.

"Is poor Jack gone?" The pirate asked motioning in the direction of the dead man.

"Aye." I answered. "His was a stomach wound."

"Bellywounds are the worst." The pirate sighed. "I have no pain in my leg and that worries me. I think when Owen looked at it this morning he had the saw in mind. Do you think he will take it?"

I was spared giving an answer, for at that moment the carpenter returned and said that Captain Teach had asked for me.

We had been cruising near Charles Town for a week, keeping well off the bar, for the waters off the shore of the Carolinas are uncommonly shallow. Captain Teach had captured several smaller vessels, but these he had not let sail after robbing them. Instead, they were anchored under the guns of the *Revenge*, ships and crew his prisoners. The last prize had been a larger ship, a brigantine bound for London, commanded by one Robert Clark.

"Princeling, I am going to put you ashore." With those words Blackbeard greeted me. He was standing near the helm of *Queen Anne's Revenge*, surrounded by some pirates and a man I had never seen before. "You and Mr. Marks here will be my ambassadors. You will meet with the town council and ask for medical supplies." Blackbeard grinned and turning to a gentleman in his thirties said, "This is the princeling, so called because his father is king of Jamaica."

"I thought the king of England ruled Jamaica," Mr. Marks said, looking me over.

"So does the king, but he is wrong. The princeling's father is the true owner. Captain Richard!" Blackbeard turned to the pirate whom he had given command of Major Bonnet's ship. "Take your longboat and four of your crew and escort my ambassadors to Charles Town. If you do not return, it shall be my pleasure to blow up every ship I have taken without first removing their crews. If you contemplate running away, princeling, then I shall personally cut the throat of your little friend below."

I said nothing, only nodding to show that I had understood. The longboat of the *Revenge* was already alongside. Richard, a friend of Gibbet and easily as cruel as he, indicated that we were to embark. Seated beside Mr. Marks on the seat in the bow of the longboat, I watched the pirate in the stern handling the tiller. Four other rascals were at the oars. I looked up to stare into the face of Blackbeard. He was laughing. Why had he sent me, I wondered? No doubt it was part of a game he was playing with me, a kind of trial he was conducting. When would he grow tired of this game, and what would happen then? He would probably cut my throat and throw me to the sharks.

"Would he blow up the ships and kill the crews?" Mr. Marks whispered to me. I watched the bent backs of the pirates rowing and the expression on Captain Richard's face. "Yes," I whispered back, "he would, and when morning came the next day, he would have forgotten that he had done it."

"An animal." Mr. Marks voice was deep with anger. "My wife is on board Captain Clark's ship."

Straight as an arrow the boat headed for the town's harbour. I let my hand dangle in the water. It was warm and pleasant. "What exactly is Blackbeard asking for?" I asked.

"A full medicine chest," Mr. Marks grumbled. "It seems they have not even bandages left."

"That is true. Will he be given it?" I asked, drawing in my hand and wetting my face. It was noon and very hot.

"Oh yes, and more if he will leave the town." We were getting near the entrance to the harbour. Some elegant houses were built along the waterside, and suddenly I realized how strange it was going to feel to be walking on land again. I turned to my companion and smiled. He was looking back at the ships where his wife was a prisoner.

Chapter 12

Charles Town

WE WERE MET WITH A WHOLE DELEGATION OF men, some carrying arms. I thought for a moment that we were going to be arrested. But Mr. Marks spoke to them and they moved away allowing us to come ashore. As I jumped unto the pier I almost fell as the solid land seemed to be moving under my sea legs.

"Heave-to," said one of the pirates who steadied me. "Thank you," I said and smiled, but I walked gingerly for quite a while until I felt my legs were obeying me again.

Mr. Marks and I were taken to the city council where he explained Blackbeard's demands. It did not take them long to agree, especially since one of Blackbeard's prisoners, Mr. Samuel Wragg, was a member of the city council.

"Is this young man a pirate?" an elderly councilman asked. He had a large, white beard, and deep in his wrinkled face, a pair of very pale blue eyes stared at me.

"No, I am a prisoner, sir. My name is William Bernard. I was taken from my father's ship by Captain Teach."

"Captain!" the councilman said sourly. "Do not give that scoundrel Blackbeard such an honest title. If we don't give him what he demands, will he do what he has promised to do?"

"Yes, he will," I said, suddenly realizing why I had been sent. My words would be much more convincing than Mr. Marks'.

"Blackbeard keeps his promises whether for good or bad. He is a strange and cruel man, but if he has said that the ships he holds will be allowed sail once you have given him what he demands, then that will be so."

"He told me," Mr. Marks pleaded, "that if the chest were not filled with medicine, he would have the heads of all his prisoners cut off and sent to the govenor. He also said that he would burn the ships. Gentlemen, my wife is among them!"

"Give him what he wants!" screamed a woman frantically.

"Calm yourself, Mrs. Wragg," the councilman said, "we shall give him what he has asked for. Will you stay here, Mr. Marks, or will you return in the boat?"

"My wife is a prisoner aboard Captain Clark's ship, so I shall return. But young Bernard here should be free to go."

"There is a boy on board whom Blackbeard has promised to kill if I do not return," I said. I was sure that Blackbeard would kill Sam if I was not in the longboat when it returned.

"But I understand he is only a slave," Mr. Marks protested. "A white man's freedom is more important than a black man's life."

I shook my head, but said nothing, for Mr. Marks would never understand that Sam was my friend, and his life as precious to me as my own. "I shall return with the boat, but I would like to be able to write to my father to tell him that I am alive."

I was given paper, pen and ink, but it was hard for me to write. The words did not come easily. I tried to explain why I had to return to the pirate ship, and ended the letter with a promise that I would try to escape as soon as I could. The elderly councilman gave me an envelope and sealed it. I wrote my father's name on the outside, and Kingston, Jamaica. The council promised that it would be given to the captain of the first ship sailing that way.

I went down to where our boat was fastened, but neither Mr. Marks nor any of the pirates were there. Some children my own age were staring down onto it, as if they expected to find blood-stains there. "Where is the crew?" I asked.

"The pirates?" one boy mumbled, staring at me with great curiosity.

"Yes," I answered, looking him up and down.

"Are you a pirate?" he asked. I decided not to answer, and instead repeated my question. "Where are the men?"

"Over there." A boy a lot younger than me pointed in the direction of a lane. "They are drinking in an inn up there." Then taking for granted that I was a pirate, he asked, "Have you ever killed anyone?"

"Dozens," I answered and sauntered in the direction of the inn. The children followed me but kept a respectful distance. A sign outside the house proclaimed the name of the establishment, King Charles Inn. An appropriate name in a place called Charles Town. The portrait of the king was so poor, I thought, the artist could have been hanged for high treason without anyone objecting.

The noise from the rowdy crowd in the inn could be heard outside. I thought briefly of entering, but decided against it and instead returned to the boat, with the children still following me.

By the boat, I sat down on the stones and dangled my feet over the side of the pier. The oars in the longboat had been laid neatly across the thwarts and the oarlocks stowed away. Shipshape and Bristol-fashioned, I thought with a grin. It was an expression I had heard Captain Teach use. He was Bristol-born and proud of it.

A girl, more courageous than the other children, asked me if there were any girl pirates. I laughed and said, "Not on board the *Queen Anne's Revenge*. Would you like to become one?" I asked.

"Not really," she said very seriously, "I just wondered. There are so few things a girl can do. If she is born poor she can only be a maid."

"Are you poor?" A silly question, for her dress and bare feet showed clearly that she was.

"Sure I am poor..." she frowned, then glancing at my clothes, she asked, "are you rich?"

I said that my father was, and asked her name.

"If your father is rich, then you are rich, too. It is the same thing." The girl looked defiantly at me, then recollecting that I had asked her name said, "Faith."

"And where are Hope and Charity?" I asked, smiling.

"They are my younger sisters." Then, maybe because I had smiled, she added, "My father was a sailor. He was drowned."

"I am sorry," I said.

"I am not. I didn't like him...he drank." Faith paused. "Maybe I am a little sorry, it must be very lonely to drown."

"Yes, that is true." I had never before thought of loneliness and drowning as in any way connected. "It must be very lonely, with the ocean so huge and you so small."

"Have you any beautiful sisters?" The girl looked so earnestly at me that I did not laugh, but merely said that I had no sisters.

"I wish I were beautiful, but I am not. Do you think I am ugly?"

I looked at her carefully. "You are not ugly," I said, "You may grow up to be beautiful."

"If you are beautiful, then a rich man may marry you even though you are poor and your father was drowned." Faith said *was drowned* almost as if it was the same as *was hanged*.

"Faith, come here!" a tough-looking woman screamed. Faith shrugged her shoulders and declared, "my mother," and left.

I nodded and wished her luck. I knew that I would remember

that conversation and I would tell Sam about the girl. She was still a child, just as I had been not so very long ago.

Shortly after the pirates came, the worse for drink. A little later, Mr. Marks arrived with a cart carrying the medicine chest. As we rowed away, Mr. Marks looked longingly towards the shore.

Chapter 13

I return to the *Queen Anne's Revenge*

"WHY DID YOU NOT STAY?" MR. MARKS ASKED AS we were being rowed back to the pirate ships. "Blackbeard would not have killed the slave boy. He would have sold him."

I shook my head. "No. He would have killed him." I don't know why, but I knew that I was right. Mr. Marks was a merchant. To him Sam was a piece of goods, and you don't throw valuable wares away, you sell them. "Captain Teach does not care for money."

"Nonsense, boy. Gold is the only thing pirates care about. Why, a true buccaneer will kill his own mother for a doubloon."

"Gold, sir, yes he does care for that. But it is to throw away, not to keep." That was true of most of the pirates. They wanted to win fortunes so they could lose them, by the turn of a card or by a woman.

"He is cruel, though. Like a weasel, he kills for the love of it." Mr. Marks stared towards the ship where his wife was held prisoner.

"That is true. He likes killing and he is in love with death. He seeks it for himself. He is always the first man to board a prize, and he never hides. I have heard him laugh when the bullets whistle close."

"You like him?" Mr. Marks asked, not bothering to hide his contempt.

I shook my head. I wanted to say I hated him, but was that true? I looked aft at Mr. Richard, who grinned knowingly as if he had understood what we were talking about. "He has been very strange to me, done me no harm when he could have, but I have no liking for him." There was no point in saying anything more, for Mr. Marks would not understand even if I explained it. Blackbeard kept me because I am what he might have been under other circumstances. That is partly why he sent me, to test me, to see if I would run away. If I had, he would have killed Sam because he said he would, and if he ever caught me again, he would kill me, too.

The pirates pulled in their oars and the longboat glided alongside the hull of the *Queen Anne's Revenge*. A line cast from above landed on Mr. Marks' head, and with a snarl of irritation, he pushed it aside. Laughing, one of the pirates grabbed it.

"So you came back." Blackbeard smiled as if he was satisfied. "Now, princeling, what would you do if I had killed your little playmate?"

"You haven't done it," I stared at Captain Teach, "so I don't have to make up my mind about it."

"How do you know that, princeling?" Blackbeard was paying no attention to Mr. Marks or the chest of medicine that had been brought aboard.

"I know you keep your word." The deck was boiling hot under my bare feet.

"That is so." Captain Teach ordered the chest to be carried to the carpenter, then noticing Mr. Marks he said, "Get on board your ship and be gone."

"But you, princeling," the pirate turned again to me, "what would you have done if I had killed the boy?"

"I don't know." I looked down at the deck, shifted my position, and looked straight in his eyes. "If I could, I would have killed you."

"Good!" Blackbeard roared with laughter, and then suddenly growing serious, he said, "Maybe I would have let you." He laughed again as if his last words contained a joke, and pushed me gently towards the bow of the ship. "Go and play with the major's little blackamoor. He is with the carpenter."

"I have been sick," Sam said to me, and indeed he looked unwell. "I had to help the carpenter cut off a man's leg," he explained in a plaintive voice. Then smiling grimly, he said, "I think I would prefer to cut off the carpenters head."

"Let us go on deck." The smell in the carpenter's "hospital" was awful.

"Did your patient die or is he alive?" I asked, glad that I had not been there for the operation.

"He is still breathing and moaning. He lost at least a bucketful of blood."

Our prizes were all heaving up anchors and unfurling their sails. Captain Teach had kept his word, and his prisoners their heads. It had all been a matter of pride.

"The carpenter told me that Blackbeard has sworn to sell me." Sam breathed deeply of the fresh air.

"Why?" I asked. "He can't. You belong to the major." I sat down in my usual place by the bowsprit.

"Oh, that is the reason." Sam smiled at the thought. "They hate each other, and Blackbeard is selling me to spite my father."

"He is mad and so is your father. Why did he leave Barbados if he had a plantation there?"

Sam shrugged. "How do I know? And what is more, I do not care...But I don't want to be sold."

"No." I shook my head. "We must get away."

"Yes, for the sake of both of us," Sam laughed. "The carpenter said that the major promised that if Blackbeard sold me, he would sell you."

"He can't sell me. I am…" I said no more. Now it was Sam who shook his head.

Sam frowned. "Have you ever heard of indenture? You are a child. The major or Blackbeard could sell you as a servant for a certain sum for you to work for eight years. The major has had two servants like that. One I knew well was no more than a child. He told me that he had been caught in the street and taken aboard a ship. He was a foolish boy, cried a good deal."

"What happened to him?" I asked. My father had no servants like that, at least not in our house.

"What happened to him? He died. The major's wife—I told you about her—she beat him to death."

"She did that?" I looked out over the sea. Our ship, the *Revenge*, and two small sloops were the only ones left at anchor. "Why did she do it?" I wanted a reason, though by now I knew that cruelty does not need one.

"I don't know. I felt sorry for him, though he was stupid. But a servant that has put his mark on an indenture is worse off than a slave. A slave has value, he can be bartered with, but an indentured servant has only the value of the work you can beat out of him."

"I would never sign," I said, watching a school of flying fish. "Never," I repeated.

"You wouldn't have to. Captain Teach could do that, or the major. Where have you been in the world, Will? A child has not much more right than a slave." Sam snorted and added "but a slave child has even less."

I glanced at my friend, remembering the whip marks on his back, and laid my hand for a moment on his shoulder. "My world was very different from this," I said indicating the pirate ship.

Then I began telling Sam about my childhood. I described the big house and my daily visits to my mother in her self-made prison. I told him about the meals I had eaten alone, or together with my father at the huge table in our diningroom. Lastly, I described Mary, the slave girl who had taken care of me, and was the only person who I was sure loved me.

"Princeling." Sam shook his head in wonder. I frowned for I hated that name. "But it is true," Sam argued. "You were a prince. Was the girl pretty?"

I did not like the question, still I tried to answer it. "I think she was, but she was more like a mother or an older sister to me."

"What was her color?" Sam looked very intently at me. "Was she black?"

I shook my head. "No. She was more your color," I finally said as I tried to conjure up a picture of Mary in my mind.

"Then she's probably your half-sister," Sam said.

Then suddenly I recalled an incident that had taken place when I was ten. When he went away to visit other islands, my father would always bring me a gift. That time he had brought me something I did not care for, and had given Mary a beautiful shawl that even I could see had been more expensive than what he had given me. I made a fuss and Mary had put the shawl away and never worn it. "Maybe," I whispered, as if telling a secret, "maybe she *is* my sister."

"Lucky for her that her father was not the major," Sam smiled.

I glanced out over the sea and suddenly so much that I had not understood became plain to me. My father had always treated Mary differently from any other slave or servant. Maybe he had good reason to. There is so much a child cannot or does not understand. I am not yet a man, I thought, but I am no longer a child.

Chapter 14

Major Bonnet's confession

THAT NIGHT CAPTAIN TEACH INVITED HANDS and Richard, who had both been promoted to captains of the sloops, and Major Bonnet, to a drunken feast. On a big table he had spread the 1,500 pounds sterling he had robbed from the ships taken outside Charles Town. It was an impressive pile, all in gold and silver. "It is a pleasant sight, isn't it?" He took a gold coin from the table and looked at it. "If I were king, I would not have my face portrayed where grubby hands could touch it." He turned to me. "Princeling, get the sack over there, and stow away the money in it." He nodded to Sam. "You help him, but if your fingers are so sticky that gold clings to them, I will cut them off. When you are finished set the table, but first bring in the silver goblets and the wine."

Quickly we gathered in the coins, and the full sack was heavy. Then Sam took out the goblets Blackbeard had stolen from the Spanish ship before it caught fire. They were made of silver and gold, engraved with pictures of birds and animals.

The wine was Frankish and of good quality. We had hardly finished pouring one round before another was called for. Of all the people on this earth, pirates must suffer most from thirst, and of a kind that cannot be quenched by water.

Isreal Hands had moments when he became more a preacher than a pirate. This happened when he became almost insensible from drink. Though he had not reached that state yet, he was not keeping himself from it. Richard, too, was drinking heavily, and only Major Bonnet was frugal with his wine.

"Major, you are not drinking. Is the wine not to your taste?" Blackbeard asked jovially.

"I want my ship back, Teach." The major sipped from his goblet. "As for the wine, I have no reason to complain."

"I cannot give it back to you since I have never taken it from you." Blackbeard grinned. "I gave Richard here the command for a short while, so that I could have the pleasure of your company. Cheers and damn our enemies." Blackbeard lifted his goblet.

"I shall sleep aboard the *Revenge* tonight." Major Bonnet lifted his goblet as well.

"As you choose to, it is your ship," Blackbeard drank. "Now, Captain Richard, here, not only brought back from the town a medicine chest but some fowl as well. You are all good, solid trenchermen, so let us at it, a bird for each."

Sam and I had set the table, and in the center was a large serving dish piled high with roasted chickens. The smell of the cooked chickens made me aware of how hungry I was. On board the *Queen's Anne's Revenge* no one ever ate well, and I realized that I had not eaten the meat of a fowl since I left Jamaica.

"Are you hungry, princeling? Here." Blackbeard handed me a leg of his chicken. Seeing this, Major Bonnet gave Sam a wing. He was now drinking heavily as well, and I guessed Sam would soon be his son again. The major sober and the major drunk were two very different persons, though I could not say I cared for either of them.

"Pirates get hanged when caught, not because our trade is more dishonest than other men's, but because we interfere with theirs. A pirate might take as a prize a slave ship and sell the merchandise it contains. He steals what is already stolen, for none of those poor blacks have walked the gangplank voluntarily. But if he is caught he is called a thief, whereas the original owners are honest merchants." Blackbeard had finished eating and pushed his plate aside. "I have no use for slavers. I sailed in one once, and the stink of rotten carcasses have been in my nose ever since."

"Somewhere in the Bible, I think, it is written that the black man must be slave to the white." Isreal Hands had now reached the state when he began to preach. He looked up at the ceiling as if searching for inspiration there.

Captain Teach grinned. "If it is written in the Book, you are sure to know it, Hands." Turning to Captain Richard he asked, "Stiles, what say you about the slavers?"

"I have never sailed in a slaver. Gibbet has, and did not like it. Most of the slaves died of sickness and so did more than half the crew. The only happy ones were the sharks that ate them. I would not touch that trade, though there is money to be earned in it, that is true enough. Piracy suits me, for we are honest knaves, we that sail under the black flag." Richard lifted his goblet in a toast and then emptied it.

"And what do you say, Major? You had slaves back in Barbados."

"Where sugar is king, slavery must be." The major hiccuped. These were obviously not his own words but an old slogan.

"You have a slave along." Captain Teach turned to look at Sam. "Would you sell him to me?"

"Samuel—that was my father's name—is a product of my own loins. I could not think of selling him." The major looked over at his son.

I noticed that the major's eyes had grown moist as he spoke. I looked at Sam and he winked at me.

"No man would sell his own son. That is understandable." Blackbeard nodded in a most emphatic manner. "But what about losing him on the turn of a card? Many a gentleman has lost his all in such a manner, without losing his good name."

"The devil's bible," Isreal Hands proclaimed. "Those who read from that book will end up roasted in the eternal fires." The pirate pushed his goblet away, still half-full of wine, and rose from the table. "The wages of sin shall be paid in eternity," he declared and left the cabin.

"Who pays those wages, the devil or God?" Captain Teach asked, grinning, and then turning to Major Bonnet he asked once more, "Will you gamble for him? Five doubloons of purest gold against that son of yours?"

I looked at the major. I knew his greed. Stede Bonnet looked first at Blackbeard, then at his son, then slowly he pointed to the heavens.

"By the name of He who rules above, I swear that Samuel Bonnet is my son and no more a slave than I am. He is a freeman of Barbados and my heir." He grabbed his goblet and as he drank, some of the wine ran down his chin. "The Almighty that pays the wages of sin is a paymaster that never stints. I have reason to know of this." Major Bonnet looked darkly at his two drinking companions.

"What do you mean by that?" Captain Richard asked, the least drunken of the party.

"My mother's maiden name was Peachell. Her father was Hugo Peachell." Suddenly remembering Samuel, he turned towards him and said, "That was your great-grandfather." Sam was smiling, but it was a bitter smile.

"My grandfather, Hugo Peachell, died the very night of the day I was born. They said there was a smell of brimstone when he died, for the devil took him as he took his master, Oliver Cromwell, perpetrator of the king's murder. He came to our island shortly after he had done his foul deed, sent there because no one wanted him in England."

"What had he done?" Richard asked, now more interested in the major's ravings.

"The word is regicide, though the more common word is murder. He, my grandfather..." the major's voice faltered for a moment, "was the wielder of the axe that cut off King Charles' head."

I looked at Captain Teach, as fierce a royalist as most of the pirates. To them, Cromwell was but another name for the devil. Blackbeard shook his head. "I have never heard that name before...Peachell. I think the man who did that deed was called something else. Was it not Dick Brandon?"

"So people think or were told. The truth is he lost the use of his right arm the very day he should have grabbed the axe. God had lamed him, and someone else had to be found to do that deed. The devil took Dick Brandon just a few months after the death of His Majesty. My grandfather was a sergeant in the parliamentary troops, and he volunteered to murder God's anointed king.

"I say God forgive him, yet I know he never will. Masked with a hood to cover his head, my grandfather swung the axe, forgetting first to ask forgiveness from his victim. But then he was not used to the trade he had just taken up. A few weeks after so great a sin, he was dispatched to Barbados, Colonel Ireton himself arranging it and paying him as well. Before he died he confessed all of this to a clergyman of his faith." Major Bonnet sighed and looked down.

I glanced at Sam. He was frowning, and I suspected this was a story he had never heard before.

"To King Charles of England, and may your grandfather roast in hell forever, Stede. Fill our glasses, princeling." Captain Teach held out his goblet and I hastened to fill it.

The toast was drunk, by Major Bonnet as well, and more toasts were made until the pirates could hardly reel to their berths. Major Bonnet did not get aboard his ship that night. As for Sam and I, we were so tired that we had only one wish—to sleep. But I did find out that he had never heard the tale of his great-grandfather before. He confessed that it rather pleased him to have so infamous a family member. When I congratulated him on his freedom, he laughed. It was the custom of the major to set him free when he was in his cups, only to retain him as a slave when he woke up sober.

Chapter 15

My friend Sam is taken away

I WOKE UP FEELING THAT SOMETHING WAS wrong. I got out of my bunk, stole a glance into the main cabin, and heard as well as saw that Blackbeard was still asleep, lying on his back and snoring with his mouth open. Captain Teach at best was not handsome, and that morning he was at his worst. I ran up on deck and my suspicion that something was wrong was verified. A hundred yards away I saw Sam rowing the little jolly-boat of the *Queen Anne's Revenge*, with Major Bonnet sitting aft surrounded by his belongings.

Why didn't he wake me to say goodbye, I wondered, feeling miserable. Then it occured to me that the major had not allowed it, for fear of waking Blackbeard. He did not trust Captain Teach and I could not blame him for that. There was a good chance that the pirate would have forgotten the promises of the night before, and kept Major Bonnet aboard the *Queen Anne's Revenge*. I watched the major climb aboard his vessel, and wondered for the tenth time at least, why he

78

had ever gone to sea. He was a born landlubber and would never become a sailor.

A little later the jollyboat returned, rowed by one of the pirates who had been sent with Richard Stiles when he was cap-tain of the *Revenge*. As he climbed over the railing, I asked him what had happened. With a look of disgust on his face he said, "That clodhopper has taken command again. He can call himself captain as much as he wants to, but he will never become one for all of that." Pausing a minute before he tied the painter, the pirate spat into the sea to show his disgust. I watched him go below to Blackbeard's cabin. He had a message from the major that would not be complimentary, I thought, and grinned.

Shortly after that, the *Revenge* weighed anchor and got under way. She set a course out to sea and as she passed near us, Sam and I waved to each other. To my surprise, tears were running down my cheeks. In all my plans for escape, Sam had always been prominent. Now I was alone, and suddenly I felt that I would never see the island of Jamaica again.

I stamped my foot in a sudden burst of rage against my fate and swore that I would get back somehow. I wiped my tears on my sleeve and raised my hand in a last salute to Sam, though I was sure he could no longer see me. When the *Revenge* was about a mile further out to sea, she changed course and headed north. The wind was a steady light breeze from the west.

"You lost your friend, princeling." Captain Teach glanced first up at the masts then out over the sea, then yawned and stretched himself. "I shan't miss his father, as big a fool as his grandfather, the regicide, probably was. Go and find Gibbens and tell him to come to the cabin, and bring Richard as well."

Both men were still in their berths, having drunk well the night before. Cursing me for waking them, they nevertheless got up and staggered off to Blackbeard's cabin. I followed them, but Captain Teach made a sign for me to stay on deck.

"What are they up to?" asked Samuel Odell, who was thick as thieves with Isreal Hands and served on his sloop.

I shrugged. I disliked the man. He and Isreal Hands were brutes, but filled with morals at the same time, a combination I did not care for. They had been in a frenzy killing the Spaniards, cutting their throats while shouting, "Death to the idolaters." Isreal Hands would hold a service on Sundays, which Samuel Odell always attended. It seemed to me that if a pirate needed a god to pray to, then the devil would have to do.

"Gibbet loaded some heavy sacks into the jollyboat last night, and rowed them over to Richard's sloop. What was in them?" Sam Odell tried to catch my eye, to make sure that he would know if I was lying when I answered.

"How should I know." I looked towards the sloop which Richard commanded. I was surprised that Gibbens had not been at the supper the night before, and thought that somehow he had fallen into disfavor with Blackbeard. Why had Hands been there? I knew that Captain Teach did not care for him. Something was up, but what?

"He will try and cheat us out of our share, is that it?" The pirate looked menacingly at me as if I was the one trying to cheat him. "Share and share alike, that is what I was told when I signed on."

"I didn't know you could write your name," I said with disgust, staring in a notherly direction and wondering if I could still see the *Revenge*.

"I put my mark on it and that is as good as a name. If he cheats us, God will punish him."

I did not laugh as I turned to stare at Sam Odell. "Do you really think He will?" I said, wondering if the pirate believed in a God who would care if one thief cheated another thief out of the loot they had stolen. Then I recalled Odell's behavior in the fight on the Spanish ship and thought to myself, *I hope they will hang you some day.*

"Share and share alike," the pirate repeated as he walked away, his brow furrowed in thought. I considered going up to the bow, but because Sam was no longer on board, I decided to climb to the masthead of the foremast.

Up there I felt free, as if I was not part of the pirate ship, but suspended in air like a bird. I looked toward land and wished I was there. Surely in Charles Town there would be someone who knew of my father and would help me to get back. But that would mean abandoning Sam, and what would happen to him when Major Bonnet was captured. I felt certain that sooner or later the major would be caught. What would happen to me if Captain Teach was caught? Would I be taken for a pirate, too? There was only one punishment for piracy and that was hanging.

"Ahoy, up there, see any ships in the offing?" I looked down to see Captain Teach with Gibbet and Richard. Slowly, I climbed down. For a moment I thought of letting myself drop into the sea, but I might have hit the deck instead. I walked aft to where the three men stood.

"The princeling is dreaming of his castle in Jamaica," Captain Teach said, looking at me with a strange smile on his face. "You cannot swim that far, so you better stay with me until I let you go."

I nodded in agreement for I had little choice but to stay. Though it was true I could not swim to Jamaica, with a bit of luck I might make it to the coast.

"I could have asked for ransom when I was in Charles Town," Richard suggested. "Though if they had known who he was they might just have held him."

"Ransom!" Blackbeard tasted the word. "What is a man worth, Richard?" Then not waiting for a response he answered his own question. "Not much, not much, yet the whole world to the man himself. I shan't sell the princeling, but will let him go free when I feel like it." With those words the pirate turned his back on all of us and stared out to sea. For a long time we stood like that and I wondered what Captain Teach was seeing. I felt certain it was not the sea but something very different.

I had seen him like that before, staring intensely at nothing at all. As suddenly as he had turned away from us, he turned back. "See that the crew is fed. After they have eaten we shall weigh anchor." The order was for Gibbet, who then glanced at Richard and ordered him back to his sloop and to be ready to sail. Then Blackbeard went below, wearing an expression on his face that made no one want to follow him.

"Where to now?" Richard asked of Gibbet. He shrugged. "I don't know. But my guess is that we will be heading north. I saw the captain studying a chart, and he had his finger on a point a degree or two north of here.

It was late in the afternoon before the *Queen Anne's Revenge* hauled up anchor and got under way. The wind had changed. It was but a breeze, very light, and coming from the southeast. That wind would die before sunset, and then an hour or two later we would catch a land breeze from the west.

I retired to my favorite spot in the bow. At least we were following the same course as Major Bonnet's *Revenge*, and there was still hope that I would see Sam again. I was lying in the shade of the big staysail, the sun was baking down, I closed my eyes and soon I was asleep.

Chapter 16

John Husk has a dream

BY MIDNIGHT THE WIND HAD DIED. SO STILL WAS it that you could have lit a candle on our mast top. There was just enough sea to make us roll gently. All sails had been furled or let down, but some of the running rigging that was not tight enough banged against the masts and booms; and yards, however well secured, still had the tendency to make an infernal noise. A ship drifting in a calm sea is not a pleasant place to be, and I have heard from those who have been caught in the doldrums for weeks that it can drive the sailors mad.

I could not sleep. I lay back against some curls of rope, and looking up at the heavens I tried to count the stars. Suddenly, it seemed as if the topmost yard on the foremast had caught fire. The light ran along the yard and down the mast to the lower yard. John Husk had told me it was called St. Elmo's fire. He also said that a ship lit by it would soon be wrecked, and he warned me that it was dangerous to look into it.

If a man's face was illuminated long enough by St. Elmo's fire,

then he was sure to die. I paid no heed to this, but stared fascinated at it. The fire jumped from the foremast to the mainmast.
Then as suddenly as it had appeared, it vanished. I crossed
myself. Had that light been lit by angels or devils, and had it
shone long enough on me to die?

At sunrise a light breeze from the east began to blow. Sails
were unfurled and foresails hoisted, and again the *Queen Anne's
Revenge* moved through the sea. When you have been long
enough on board a ship, you cannot help but feel a kind of loyalty
to the vessel. *Queen Anne's Revenge* was fast, maybe a little tender, too quick almost to obey the helm, but the kind of vessel that
was not difficult for a sailor to love. Her frame was made of oak,
but her planking was light, which might have been the reason she
was a little tender. Under press of the wind she would lean a little too far over.

Though all the materials that go into building a ship are but
dead things—copper, wood, lead, iron—the vessel itself is alive.
A living being you can love, and sometimes when the sea is
rough, you can hate as well.

That morning I did not hate *Queen Anne's Revenge*, even
though she was my prison. I wondered where we were sailing to,
if we were just looking for prizes or if Blackbeard had something
else in mind. The valuables we had taken had all been put on
board Richard's sloop. Why? I could not find an answer.

I glanced back at the two sloops that followed in our wake.
Could Sam and I have sailed one of them? No, they were too big,
possibly thirty or even forty tons. What we needed was a smaller
boat, but she would have to be seaworthy for Jamaica was far
away. Suddenly I realized that I had been daydreaming as if Sam
was still aboard. I stared ahead, hoping to see Major Bonnet's ship
in the offing. There were no sails visible. The sea stretched empty
to the thin line of the horizon where it met the sky.

By noon the breeze died again and the *Queen Anne's Revenge* hardly moved. Sails were furled, and by now the waves were so gentle that the sea had become a mirror. We had little food on board, and the men were hungry. The cook made up a dish of everything eatable left in the galley, but it was not a very appetizing stew. I did not eat any, neither did Blackbeard. His belly was still filled with chicken, whereas mine was empty.

"We are too many, we must lighten our crew. Nor do we need a ship of war like this one." Captain Teach was talking to Richard and Gibbet. "I have made a list of those I want to keep."

"*Queen Annes's Revenge* is a stout ship. I would hate to lose her." Gibbet glanced around the cabin. "You won't get quarters like this aboard the sloops."

"She needs more water than there is where we are going. Here!" Blackbeard pointed to a place on the chart that was lying on the table. "That is Topsail Inlet. We will beach her there."

"Someone with big ears is listening." Gibbet pointed towards me. I was in the corner of the cabin, and it was true enough, I was listening. "Princeling, go on deck and whistle for some wind." Blackbeard looked at me and added, "Maybe the time has come for us to part."

I obeyed but said nothing. Up on deck I drifted over to a group of pirates who were playing dice. I watched them for a while, but an old fellow told me to go away because I was a Jonah that brought ill luck. At the bow of the ship I sat down in my usual place. The time for us to part, I thought, was long ago when Sam was still on board.

Captain Teach had some new plan, one I did not fit into. What would he do? Could he sell me into slavery? I had written a letter to my father. Surely he would do something, but what if that letter had never reached him? Many ships were lost at sea and some were taken by pirates. I felt so sad and miserable that tears ran down my cheek. I wiped my face and said to myself, "William Bernard, don't be a child!"

As I looked out over the ocean, I saw the color of the sea change. First far out, then closer and closer, and then the wind caressed my face. It was a good breeze, one that promised to blow steadily and not die at sunset. A few moments later pirates were aloft unfurling sails, and soon the *Queen Anne's Revenge* heeled over gently as she raced ahead on what was to be her last voyage.

There is no music lovelier than the sound of a ship cleaving the waters, and no better place to hear it than in its bow. I lay over the bowsprit, my head so far out that I could look down on the water as it parted in a stream of white bubbles forming two little waves, one to port, one to starboard.

Two hands grabbed my ankles and pulled me back into the ship. It was John Husk. He was laughing. "I thought of shoving you the other way to keep company with the sharks."

"You didn't." I said, "Why should you drown me?"

"Maybe I wouldn't." John Husk sat down beside me. "We are going into some inlet as we need both food and water. Can you swim, princeling?"

I nodded. I hated the name Blackbeard had given me, and I felt like saying "my name is William," but I didn't.

"I dreamt last night that I died." John Husk looked mournfully away for a moment. "I think my time is up, and so is Blackbeard's. It was a grand fight. I saw it plainly though my eyes were closed in sleep."

"Did you see Captain Teach dying as well?" I asked, wondering if in our dreams truth is revealed to us.

John Husk nodded. "And so did Gibbet. Blackbeard was all bloody, standing by the helm, and Gibbet lying at his feet." The pirate frowned. "But it wasn't on board the *Queen Anne's Revenge*, and that was strange, but in some smaller boat."

"Captain Teach has some plan, but I don't know what it is. Do you know where Topsail Inlet is?" I asked.

"Not far from here in the northern part of the Carolinas." John Husk glanced towards the west where land was just visible.

"What I want to say to you is this: when we get near land, near enough that you can reach it without drowning, you must swim ashore." The pirate rose. "Give me your hand."

I stretched my right arm up to him. He put two gold doubloons in my hand and then closed my fingers gently over them. "They might be useful. I think I shall have no use for gold any longer." Then he walked away and did not look back. I opened my hand and looked at the two golden coins, then hid them as well as I could inside my scanty clothing.

Chapter 17

The wreck of the *Queen Anne's Revenge*

SEVERAL HOURS BEFORE SUNSET WE CHANGED course, due west straight for the coast. The land is low in the northern part of the Carolinas, swampy and uninhabited along the coast. The sea was changing its color, growing light as it became shallower. Some sails had been furled and only the largest of the foresails was still raised. But we were still sailing fast enough to lose our mast if we went aground. Captain Teach was at the helm, staring ahead, a grim smile on his face. Gibbet and Roberts were standing near him. Gibbet went to the bulwark and looked into the sea and then at his captain. "It is getting very shallow."

"It won't get deeper where we are going." Blackbeard grinned. "Though I have been told that Topsail Inlet has depth enough for something her size."

"It will soon be high water and this is a spring tide. If you put her aground now, she won't get free again before the moon is full once more." The carpenter glanced at the sails that were still up. "If I were you I would take in some canvas."

"I thank you for your advice, even though I won't take it, Mr. Roberts. By the way, have you killed your patients? Or are some of them so eagerly hanging onto life that even your doctoring can't finish them?"

"Those who were meant to live are alive," the carpenter grumbled. "As for the others, no one can fight the reaper. One of them will need a new leg, and I have been making it."

"Last time you made one, it was in the shape of a dolphin. What will it be this time?" Blackbeard turned to look at the carpenter for a moment. "If I shall ever need one, make mine the image of the devil."

"A peg leg will do for him." The carpenter walked away, and I thought I heard him mumble, "and the same would do for you as well." But I might have been mistaken.

"What would you rather lose, an arm or a leg, Gibbens?" Blackbeard asked.

The pirate frowned as he thought over the question. Then finally he said, "A leg, that is if it was beneath the knee, Teach."

"Aye, Gibbens, beneath the knee . . . if above you are done for. Still it is best to keep both arms and legs."

I could see plainly now where the land was broken by the inlet, and felt the wind shifting and growing weaker. Captain Teach glanced up at the masts and ordered the topsails set. Gibbet bellowed his captain's command, and four of the pirates went aloft.

"The governor of this country," Blackbeard nodded towards land, "is a gentleman who knows the value of a doubloon. His name is Charles Eden, and if he has ever been in that place, he was the snake. We can do business with him. We will take the king's pardon."

"What about that sloop?" Gibbet turned and looked towards the larger of the boats which Richard Stiles commanded. "She flew the English flag when we took her."

"You must have forgotten, Mr. Gibbens. She flew Spanish colors." Captain Teach grinned. "I hope it is your memory, not your eyesight, which has become faulty."

"Oh, yes, I recall it now. She was Spanish to be sure. An enemy of our beloved king." Gibbet grinned as well. "I am sure that there is no one on board here who would not swear to that," he said, looking directly at me. I said nothing. I knew the home-port of the sloop had been Port Royal in Jamaica, and she had flown the colors of Britain. Her crew had been set adrift in their ship's boat and crowded it had been, for it was not much larger than our jollyboat.

"I think we will set the princeling adrift soon. He will have to find his own way back to his kingdom. He won't tell a lie, so it is best that no one asks him anything." Blackbeard glanced at me for a moment, but as we were very near the inlet he looked ahead again. Gibbet frowned and mumbled, "I know a surer way to keep people from telling either lies or the truth." Then he made a motion with his hand across his neck.

As the *Queen Anne's Revenge* entered Topsail Inlet, I could feel its keel touch the sandy bottom. The wind was blowing a little harder now, and the ship was doing at least four or five knots. Passing a low, sandy island to our starboard, Captain Teach steered directly towards another, slightly larger island. I held on to the railing as the *Queen Anne's Revenge* went aground. The masts held, but the ship had gone so far up on the beach that she leaned over. Blackbeard ordered all sails furled, and was quickly obeyed.

Hands steered his smaller sloop alongside ours and beached her as well. Richard Stiles in the larger of the sloops, went into the wind and let go her anchor. I ran forward. The bow of the ship was but a few feet from the land. Land it could hardly be called, for it was only a sandy reef. I felt a longing to stand once more on solid ground and thought of jumping down.

But then one of the pirates asked me if I knew why Blackbeard had run the ship aground. "If it is because he wants to clean the bottom, he should not have done it at a spring tide. It will be hard to get her afloat again."

I shrugged my shoulders and said that I did not know what Captain Teach had planned, though I knew perfectly well by now that he planned to abandon the larger ship. Beyond the island on which we were stranded, I could see the mainland. It, too, was low and swampy and seemed deserted of human habitation. A flock of seagulls was circling our masts, looking to scavenge some food. They had little chance of that, as the larders of the *Queen Anne's Revenge* were bare.

I had not forgotten Gibbet's threatening gesture. I still wore the knife at my belt, and swore to myself that I would sell my life dearly. I understood what Blackbeard was up to. He and the men he had selected were going to abscond with the treasure. Then they would take the "king's pardon." That would be simple enough if the governor, Mr. Eden, was the kind of man that Captain Teach had hinted he was. What was going to happen to the pirates left behind? What was going to happen to me?

The longboat had been lowered and was floating alongside. Gibbet and some of the younger pirates boarded it and rowed over to the anchored sloop. Soon it returned, empty. Now I noticed that Blackbeard, as well as the pirates surrounding him, were all armed.

The pirates who were to be left behind had not understood what was happening. They could not take in the fact that they were to be marooned on this little sandy reef of an island.

Blackbeard pointed to the jollyboat that was lying upside-down on the deck. Owen Roberts ran over to it, an axe raised in his hand, and hacked in several boards, rendering the boat useless. One by one the pirates climbed over the bulwark and down into the longboat. Blackbeard was the last to embark. He stood for a moment, arrogantly staring at the men he was leaving behind, a cocked pistol in each hand. One of the pirates grabbed a wooden pin and ran towards him. Blackbeard waited and then fired one of his pistols. The pirate fell at his feet, the heavy pin rolling down the deck. Then Captain Teach stuck his pistols into his belt and swung himself over the bulwark.

The castaways all ran to the bulwark and looked down at the longboat already pulling away, with Captain Teach at the tiller. One of the oarsmen was John Husk. He looked up at me, then shrugged his shoulders as if to say, "I cannot help it."

When the boat was a few lengths away, Blackbeard ordered the men to stop rowing. Then he turned to look for the last time at the *Queen Anne's Revenge*. Noticing me at the railing he raised his hand in a salute and shouted, "Go and claim your kingdom, princeling! I shall stake mine out here." Then he ordered the men to pull at their oars, and the longboat shot rapidly towards the sloop, where Gibbens and Stiles waited for him.

The pirates left behind suddenly understood their fate. Some of them ran to get pistols, but before they managed to load them, Captain Teach was aboard the sloop and the men were hoisting the sails. I looked at the pirate that Blackbeard had shot. Blood was still trickling from his wound. Then I looked at the jollyboat. Could it be fixed, I wondered, for Owen Roberts had been the only one with a carpenter's skill amongst us. How was I going to claim my kingdom now?

Chapter 18

A long dark night

THE SLOOP WITH THE TREACHEROUS BLACK-
beard on board was already out of sight. The furious men left
marooned aboard the wreck needed to vent their anger on someone. "There is his puppy," one of the pirates screamed, pointing
to me.

"I had nothing to do with it," I said, retreating towards the
bow of the ship. "He left me as well."

"Seize him!" shouted an elderly pirate I had always thought of
as one of the more decent among the men. I started to run
towards the foremast, meaning to climb it. But a pirate grabbed
me, lifted me off my feet, and turned me upside down. The two
gold doubloons fell from their hiding place onto the deck. The
sight of the gold made the pirate let go of me and I fell onto the
planks, head first. Stunned, I watched the pirates fight over the
coins. Then the elderly pirate, spying my gold cross and chain,
rushed up to tear it from my neck.

This made me realize that if I did not act quickly, I would be killed. I ran for the shrouds and made my way up the ratlines to the crosstree. Here I paused, and looked down.

Some of the pirates were still arguing over the ownership of my two doubloons, but one had drawn his pistol and was aiming at me. I ducked behind the mast as he fired, but the bullet went wild. Now another wanted to prove himself a better marksman, but his pistol did not fire. It was only a flash in the pan. I drew my knife in case any of them decided to climb the rigging after me.

But none did, for suddenly they realized the ship was theirs to plunder. They all crowded down to Blackbeard's cabin. I did not believe they would find any gold there, but was thankful for the diversion. As they ransacked the accommodation aft, I looked out over the swamp that divided the key we were marooned on from the mainland. Could I make my way across it? There would be places where I would have to swim. But what about alligators? Was it infested with them? I had to get away from the ship, that was certain, for it would be less dangerous to keep company with the reptiles than the pirates.

As I knew, the pirates found no gold in Blackbeard's cabin, but they had discovered what was second-best—barrel of rum and a dozen bottles of wine. The young pirate who had caught me was wearing Blackbeard's hat. The barrel was quickly spiked, and then the drinking started. The thirst of a pirate is not quenched until there is either no more to drink or he has passed out.

At first there was singing, and attempts to do some shooting. A flight of pelicans was aimed at but none of the birds was hit. Then a few shots were fired up at me. Soon the pirates got tired of shooting. I counted seventeen in the brotherhood below. Captain Teach had selected those he took with him carefully, as what was left was only the rabble. He had treated me kindly, I had to admit, but why had he left me at the mercy of these men? I made myself as comfortable as I could. I did not dare climb down.

The sun set golden red, for a moment turning the sea purple. Thoughts of home, my father, and Mary came to me. Would I ever see them again? Then I thought of Sam and realized how much I missed him. Where was he now? My cheeks grew wet as I cried.

One by one the stars came out, shining crystals in the darkness of the night. What were they? Mary thought they were lanterns from paradise. I had learned from my tutor that there were millions of suns far, far away. Stars are cold and lonely, but the moon is friendly, and I longed for it to rise. The pirates were still drinking, and they had brought out a lantern. Two of them had gotten into an argument and a fight, to the amusement of the others. I looked towards land hoping that somewhere in the darkness there were houses, homes, other human beings. But I could see no lights. Strange birds cried, and one sounded almost like a child in pain, or the ghost of a soul lamenting what it had lost.

I wanted to climb down, even to be allowed to sit among the pirates, but I knew that would be foolish of me. Up here in the crosstrees I was safe, at least until morning.

The shrouds that run from the chainplates in the side of the ship up to the crosstrees steady the lower mast. From the crosstrees, other shrouds run to the topmast to steady it when sails are unfurled. The crosstrees are sturdy, made of oak with a decking of timber. On this little platform I was not too uncomfortable, though the ship's slant to the port side made me fear that if fell asleep I might fall down on the deck.

At last the moon rose, turning the water to silver in its ghostly light. The sharp, piercing cries of the shore birds made the desolate landscape even more lonely and sad.

The moon had almost set when I fell asleep, and I almost slid off my high perch. I woke as my shoulder hit the shrouds to the topmast and my feet were dangling in empty space. Had I not wakened, the rest of me would soon have followed. I felt a loose line next to the mast. It was a halyard that no one had bothered to fasten. I pulled up enough of it to bind myself to the mast, and now when I slept I would not fall off my post.

The pirates were silent. Their little lamp had drained its oil and died. My eyes closed once more, and I dreamt I heard Captain Teach's voice saying "princeling." I was not on the *Queen Anne's Revenge* but on another ship. Blackbeard, Gibbet, Owen Roberts, and Richard Stiles were there, sitting in a circle on the deck drinking. John Husk was there as well, with his lute in his hands.

Captain Teach lifted his gold and silver goblet and declared, "I should not have let the princeling go but taken him with us. He was our luck. I did not know it, but now I feel we have lost it. So the devil can make ready our berths in hell, for I fear we are coming."

"I wish in that case that I had killed him." Gibbet declared.

"Mr. Gibbens, you did not, and that proves he was our luck." Captain Teach looked down into his goblet as he muttered, "he was a lamb not to be slaughtered. Had I a son, he would have been like him." Then looking up towards the crosstrees of his ship, he lifted his goblet as if toasting something up there. I felt terribly sad as the images disappeared. In the darkness I heard the voice of John Husk singing. "The wind blows free across the sea, and brothers all we be." Then I woke. In the east, a slight light was showing on the horizon. Soon it would be morning.

Chapter 19

Sam and I are together again

AS THE SUN ROSE A SLIGHT BREEZE BEGAN TO blow from the southeast. No one stirred. It was still early, and considering the amount the pirates had drunk the night before, I thought it safe to climb down from my perch. I was not only hungry but thirsty as well. There should still be some water on board.

Standing on the topmost ratline, I took one look out over the sea before descending. In the distance I saw a sail. A ship was coming from the south, heading for Topsail Inlet. I climbed back up on the crosstree platform to get a better view. Yes, there was no doubt about it, she was heading in our direction. She had all sails set, and I knew her rigging. It was the *Revenge*. I felt so sure of it that I almost shouted Sam's name out loud.

What was she doing here? I knew that Major Bonnet had talked about cruising for prizes near Bermuda. But Captain Teach had deemed it foolish, for two of the king's frigates were stationed in the harbor of that island. Had he changed his mind?

My head was full of questions. I watched the *Revenge* approaching, fearing all the time that she might go about and head out to sea again. Topsail Inlet even at low tide had water enough for the *Revenge*, but still…

At last there was no doubt. I could see the men on board getting the anchor ready, and I thought I saw Sam standing aft near the helm. As the ship came in through the inlet I stood up, shouting and waving my arms wildly. The *Revenge* came into the wind, her sails backed, and when she lay completely still, her anchor was dropped. Now I realized that she was towing a small sloop of about ten tons, a pretty little craft.

Some of the pirates on board the *Queen Anne's Revenge* had woken and they, too, shouted and waved towards Major Bonnet's ship. Now I could plainly see Sam, and he recognized me. We called out each other's names, and then I decided it was safe for me to descend. Few of the pirates could swim, and with the jollyboat's timber stowed in, they must have been wondering how and if they would ever reach land.

Suddenly I had changed from a scapegoat into someone who might be of help. The pirate who had stolen my gold cross came up to me and, with a lame excuse, handed it back to me. "He will take us along?" he asked, pointing in the direction of the *Revenge*.

"I suppose so," I answered, on purpose a little doubtfully.

"I am as good a sailor as ever has shipped out of Bristol." The pirate pointed towards the *Revenge*, where the sailors were furling the square sails on the foremast. "Now look at the monkeys there, landlubbers all, playing sailors. If the wind rose to a storm they would all go below and say their prayers, rather than climb the rigging and save the ship."

"You are from Bristol?" I asked. "So is Captain Teach, I believe."

"I wouldn't know in what unfortunate town his keel was laid, but I can tell you where that blackguard will end up! That is if the devil will take him in. Though he is not particular about who he lets into hell, Blackbeard might be a bit too much even for that place. He stole our money!"

"Major Bonnet is coming across. We better throw down a companion ladder aft, where the water is deepest," I said, wondering how quickly stolen money became the sacred property of the thief.

"Aye, aye, sir." the pirate responded with a grin, and went aft to do as I had asked. I smiled at the thought that last night he would have killed me, and today he is willing to obey my order. I went aft. It was now near low tide and it was a very low ebb. In a spring tide the tidal flow is greatest, and just as high tide is highest, then so is low tide, or ebb tide, lowest. More than half of the *Queen Anne's Revenge* was dry on the sandbank.

"Ahoy, what has happened?" the Major called as he tied his boat's painter to the lowest rung of the ladder. "Where is Captain Teach?"

Leaning over the bulwark I shouted back, "He has gone in the bigger of the sloops. He has deserted us."

"Well, that is no ill fortune," Major Bonnet grumbled, as with great difficulty he climbed the companion ladder.

In the boat below I could see Sam's face, and I laughed and then held out my hand to help his father aboard. "Where has Blackbeard gone to?" Major Bonnet asked, puffing from the exertion.

"I don't know, sir. He took half his crew with him, and all that was of value on board. I think he was going to take the king's pardon."

"So he, too, has heard the rumor that we are at war with Spain again. I shall also take the pardon and then we shall be honest privateers again, flying not the black rag but the banner of king and country." Major Bonnet laughed as he turned to the pirates who had all drawn near. "If you will serve me, you shall not be sorry for it, for each man shall get his fair share of the booty."

The men gave him a cheer and declared that they were more than ready, especially if he would feed them. They were, as one of them said, "faint with hunger."

A hand was laid on my shoulder, and I turned to see Sam. We stood just staring at each other, until finally Sam said, "I thought I should never see you again."

"I, too," I nodded, "We did not even say goodbye."

"My father would not let me. He was afraid that Blackbeard would find out we were leaving."

"I know, I guessed that was the reason." Sam and I had moved a little away from the pirates, who were all surrounding the major and proclaiming their loyalty to him.

"The small boat you towed? Where does it come from?" I asked.

"It was a drifter we found at sea. It must have broken its mooring." Sam lowered his voice. "You think it could sail the ocean?"

"Maybe. She is halfdecked and I think sound enough." I glanced towards the little cutter. She had a long bowsprit, which gave her a bold appearance. "Are her sails on board?"

Sam only nodded, for now Major Bonnet was ready to return to his own ship. He called us as he was climbing down the ladder. We and a few of the pirates boarded the boat and were rowed across to the *Revenge*. The rest of the pirates would be fetched later.

Sam had been elevated to the position of son again, but he felt far from certain how long that would last. "My father is at present in good humor. He talks about returning to Barbados as soon as he gets a sackful of Spanish doubloons. I doubt if he will ever get the smell of one. The only prize we have taken was a small sloop loaded with hardly anything worth stealing. It had a live pig on board which we slaughtered, and we took what else there was of food. Oh, yes, there were four kegs of rum as well."

"Some of the booty that was on board the *Queen Anne* should rightly belong to your father," I said. Sam and I were watching the longboat returning with the rest of the pirates.

"Not some of it," Sam laughed. "According to my father, it should all be his. If he ever catches Captain Teach, he will have him drawn and quartered."

"There is no honor among thieves," I said, laughing as well. "But I doubt if he has the courage to face Blackbeard should they ever meet up again."

"No, courage is not his strong point. But that is one of the few traits I don't hold against him, for I am not very brave myself."

"Only a fool would boast about his courage," I said, recalling that I had cried when sitting on the crosstree the night before. Now that Sam and I were together again, everything seemed possible. I looked aft at the little cutter swaying gently on its painter. A handsome little craft it was. Sam and I could easily manage it. Sam's gaze had followed mine to the little boat. When he looked at me, I knew we were thinking the same thing.

Chapter 20

Major Bonnet's supper

THE PIRATES BROUGHT A DOZEN BOTTLES OF wine from the *Queen Anne's Revenge* and presented them to Sam's father as a gift, hoping to gain his indulgence. He was pleased enough, and that evening he gave his crew one of the kegs of rum to drink.

As soon as we had come on board we had been given some biscuits and salted beef. The biscuits were filled with worms and the salt meat was so briny that I must have drunk a gallon of water after I ate it. By evening I was really looking forward to a real meal. The major promised that we would have roasted pork that evening with potatoes found on board the little cutter. No one, not even slaves on a sugar plantation, eats as poorly as sailors do. Often ships become derelict and drift in the ocean because their crews have died, or are too sick to set sail.

The captain's cabin of the *Revenge* was not very grand compared to the one on board Blackbeard's ship. Still, it was comfortable enough, with a table that could seat at least eight. We dined alone, the major, Sam, and I. A pirate who had been a servant in his house on Barbados served us. Major Bonnet had already finished one bottle of wine, just to taste its quality, he said, before we sat down. He opened a second and poured wine for us both. It tasted good to me, especially since I was still thirsty from my bout with the salty beef.

"To the death of our enemies," Major Bonnet declared, lifting his glass. Sam and I dutifully followed and drank to the death of our enemies. I wondered who mine were, and if my host was one of them.

Meat was brought, and indeed it was fresh pork and potatoes, as many as we could stuff inside us. That was more than a few in my case, for I had not eaten properly for nearly a week.

"Did Blackbeard starve you?" Major Bonnet asked. He was doing more drinking than eating, and had already brought another bottle to the table.

"No, sir. We had very little food on board and even our water was running out. When we had food I ate as well as he did." I found myself defending Captain Teach. After all, he had treated me more decently than I could have expected.

"Do you know where he went?" Major Bonnet leaned forward. "One of his men said that he was heading for Ocracoke Inlet."

"That may be true, he was heading north after he got out to sea." I frowned, wondering why the major had asked.

"I carry twice the firepower now that he does." The major grinned and drank. "If we should meet again, I would be doing the talking and he the listening."

"Why bother?" Sam asked and looked at his father. The major's expression changed, the grin disappeared, and a look of anger, or hatred, disfigured it.

"That is your mother's blood talking. Blackbeard humiliated your father. You should be eager to revenge me." The major shouted and then filled his glass with wine and almost emptied it in one, long draught.

"He may not have gone to Ocracoke Inlet," I said, trying to draw the major's attention from his son, who I thought stood a good chance of loosing his parent once more, and getting a master instead.

"If he is going there, then he is heading for a city called Bath where he can take the king's pardon," Major Bonnet muttered, and looked grimly into his glass as if he could see Capain Teach's face reflected there. "He stole what wasn't his."

I didn't bother to tell him that I thought the treasure on board Blackbeard's sloop was all stolen, and did not belong to either of them. Instead, I asked if it really was true that his maternal grandfather had been the man who wielded the axe on King Charles' neck.

"Oh, that is true enough, I have no doubt about it, and it has been the curse of the family ever since." The major sighed, looking at Sam. "Even this poor youngster may be under the curse of God for what his great grandfather did." Sam tried to look as if it worried him, which I doubt that it did.

"To shed the blood of the God-anointed is the greatest sin any man can commit. I curse Hugo Peachell, and wish he had been born without hands." The major's glass was empty, and when he had filled it once more, so was the bottle.

"You really think that God cares?" I asked, for I could not for a moment believe it.

"In seven generations we shall be cursed because of Hugo's crime." Major Bonnet sighed. "My wife could bear no children, I have no son." Sam shook his head without his father noticing it.

"My wife is not well." The major growled. "I think she is mad. In all of this, I feel the hand of the Almighty." The major emptied his glass and then looked around for another bottle and ordered Sam to open it. There had been a dozen bottles in all, and now half of them were gone.

"Did you ever hear of a versemaker called John Milton?" Major Bonnet lowered his voice as if he was telling a secret.

"No, I have not heard of him, but then I am very ignorant. My father was sending me to England to be educated," I answered, lowering my voice as well.

"He was a friend of that archfiend, Cromwell. He hated the king like the devil hates God. He urged Cromwell to take the life of King Charles."

The major nodded several times to emphasize what he was saying. "When the time came for the rascals to cut off the head of the God-anointed, Milton begged for a place on the scaffold. When the axe fell, he stood so near that two drops of the royal blood hit his eyes. What do you think happened then?" Major Bonnet, who had been whispering, suddenly bellowed the last words. I shook my head to indicate that I was ignorant of Mr. Milton's fate.

"Blind, my child! Two drops of royal blood and he was as blind as the bat that flies in the night!" Sam's father grabbed the bottle that his son had opened and filled his glass. Then seeing that ours were empty, he poured wine into them as well. Then he raised his glass high and indicated that we should do the same.

"To King Charles, second son of His Majesty, King James, Sovereign Lord of Great Britain." Major Bonnet drank slowly and deeply, then he held his glass for a moment in front of his face. We followed his example as best as we were able to.

"If King Charles is only a second son, why was he king?" I asked.

"His older brother died, and more was the pity for he was an able lad. He had a grand teacher who taught him all he knew—that old sea rover, Sir Walter Raleigh—and no better sailor has ever trod a deck." The major poured himself more wine, and toasted the dead son of King James as well. Then he started muttering about his own wife. It was as if he suddenly remembered her, and needed a few more glasses to help him overcome that recollection.

It was well past midnight when the major collapsed. By then there were only two bottles left. Sam and I carried him to his berth, and then went up on deck. As I climbed the ladder I could hear him being sick, and wondered if he would drown in the sea of wine he was throwing up. I called to Sam and asked if we should help him, but he shook his head.

The moon was nearly set. A few clouds were in the west, but in the east the sky was clear and starfilled. Most if not all the pirates were as drunk as their captain, and some of them were sleeping on deck. I looked aft to the little cutter that was gently swaying in the tide. There was a weak breeze, not much wind but enough. I looked at Sam, and understanding, he smiled. "Let me see if I can forage some food, enough for a day or two," he said. "We must be quick and be out of sight before dawn."

But first, I held out my hand. Sam grabbed it and we sealed our plan. At last we were going to make our escape.

Chapter 21

We escape

I WAS GETTING THE TWO FORESAILS READY ON the little cutter while Sam foraged for food on board the *Revenge*. I thought it best not to hoist the mainsail while we were right under the larger ship. With the jib and staysail set we could glide away quietly, and then haul up the mainsail once we were distant enough away not to be heard. Sam let down a big basket, that included the bottles of wine that his father had not managed to drink before he passed out. A little later when a keg of rum came down, I was going to protest, but Sam whispered, "Water". He had filled the empty keg with water for us to drink. Finally, Sam climbed down the companion ladder, holding in his hand the rope that had secured the little cutter to the *Revenge*.

The tide was outgoing and the cutter, now free, drifted slowly away. We hoisted jib and staysail, and the little boat began to obey the helm. I steered for the inlet, expecting any moment for someone in the *Revenge* to hail us. But all was silent.

As we glided through Topsail Inlet, Sam hoisted the mainsail, and I left the tiller for a moment to help pull on the halyard, in order to tighten the sail. Left with no one at the helm the little cutter went immediately into the wind, which was just as well, because it enabled us to set the sail well.

A light breeze blew from the west, and as we headed out to sea, it was a fair wind for us. Close to the coast there are sandbanks everywhere, and to be safe I kept the course until the coast was barely in sight. Then I tightened the sheets, trimming the sails, and changed course due south. There was no compass on board, but by following the coast we would be heading south. How we would ever manage to reach Jamaica without compass or charts I did not give a thought.

Slowly, the sky in the east became golden, and then the sun rose. We were now several miles south of Topsail Inlet and well out of sight from the *Revenge*. I had a drink of water. It tasted of rum but still it quenched my thirst.

We had food for no more than a few days, for the larders of the *Revenge* had not been well stocked. One of the biscuits was so hard I could hardly chew it, but at least it had no worms in it.

"You know where they come from?" Sam was trying to chew one as well. I shook my head for I had no idea. "From England. My father said they eat them in their navy. There was a sack of them on board the little sloop we took. My father said such biscuits could keep for a voyage to China and back."

I spat out what I had in my mouth as half a worm wriggled in the biscuit I held in my hand.

"There will be some leftover potatoes and pork for dinner. Would you like a potato now?" Sam asked.

"No, I want to get as far south as we can, before we have to anchor up and go ashore for food and water. If only we had some money. I have this little gold cross. Maybe I can sell it." I held out the cross on its broken chain.

"I have my patrimony." Sam grinned and took out a leather purse and opened it for me to see what it held: a mixture of some copper and silver coins and even one or two gold doubloons.

"Your patrimony?" I said surprised. "Did your father give it to you?"

Sam laughed and closed the purse. "The only patrimony he would give me would be more stripes on my back if he caught me. But he won't catch me. I will kill myself first. I stole it ... no, I took it in payment for the beatings he has given me."

"You were right, too," I said, "and he shan't catch us." The word patrimony stayed in my mind. I had never heard it before and asked Sam what exactly it meant.

"It is whatever you inherit from your father, land—money, or," Sam paused for a moment, "slaves."

The wind changed, blowing now form the northeast. I let out the mainsail a little and Sam did the same to the two foresails. Ahead I could see what Captain Teach had called Cape Fear. The water is very shallow there and I kept a course well out to sea from it. The wind had freshened a little, and our cutter was throwing the water aside as it forged through the sea. It was a long time since I had felt as happy as at that moment.

Near midnight the wind had become very light, and as usual when that happens, unsteady as well. It kept changing from east to north, which meant we had to keep resetting our sails. Finally, just before it died completely, it shifted to southeast. There was enough sea running to make the boom swing back and forth, so we lowered the mainsail. Sam was at the halyards, and when the sail was almost down he let go the peak halyard. I was folding the sail when the gaff fell and hit me. I almost passed out, and had a lump on my head for several days afterwards. Sam kept saying he was sorry, but he wasn't half as sorry as I was.

We had been too busy sailing to eat. Now in the still night, we made a feast of the meat and potatoes left over from the night before. Sam managed with my knife to open one of the bottles of wine. We had no glasses, or for that matter plates or forks, so we drank from the bottle. Sam handed it first to me and I held it up.

"To the death of our enemies," I shouted and put it to my mouth. Sam laughed and when I handed it to him he repeated the toast, imitating the voice of major Bonnet.

"I wonder," he said, chewing on a piece of meat, "why my father became a pirate. He was not rich like your father, far from it. But he was not poor either. He was comfortably well off. True his wife was a horror, a vixen. He should have taken the whip to her instead of me. But he was afraid of her, almost as much as the house slaves were. Strangely enough, she did not treat me badly, and once or twice she saved me from a beating. She spoke to me more politely than she did to her husband, and it was she, not the major, who insisted that I should learn to read and write."

"You said she was beautiful. What family did she come from? Was she Spanish or English?" I asked.

"She came from a family of very early settlers of Spanish blood. It was whispered that her great-grandmother's color was not unlike my mother's. The family was no longer rich. I was taken once to their house, and it was almost a ruin. The roof leaked and the garden was overgrown, but I could see it must once have been very grand." Sam took another swig from the bottle. "Maybe the story about her great-grandmother had some truth to it, and that is why she treated me as she did."

The wine made us sleepy, and I tied the tiller and let the boat drift. On the first night of our freedom, we soon were asleep. The last thought I had before my eyes closed was that Captain Teach would have thought it right what we had done.

I woke as the sun rose. A gull was sitting on the top of our mast. I looked towards land that was only a bluish haze in the horizon. A slight breeze was blowing northeast. I woke Sam and we each ate another of the horrible biscuits, making sure first that there were no worms in them. Then we hauled up sails again and I steered southwest, as I wanted to get nearer to the coast.

We sailed south all that day and during the night. I did not want to head for the coast until we were well south of Charles Town. We passed the town at noon, and in the afternoon I spotted an inlet that looked both wide and deep. We had no dinghy to row ashore in, so we would have to swim or wade after we anchored.

I changed course, west toward land. Sam, who was staring at the coastline, suddenly said, "Will, remember that I am your slave."

"What do you mean?" I asked, surprised.

"A free man of my color would have to carry documents to prove it. If anyone asks, say I am your slave."

I nodded, but said nothing.

Chapter 22

The old man

AS WE PASSED THROUGH THE INLET, WE TOOK
down the staysail and Sam got the anchor ready. It was not a real
anchor at all but some pieces of iron held together by a chain. But
it was heavy enough, and it would hold the cutter if the wind
was not too strong. One of the pieces of iron was a part of a
plough, which made me think that the cutter had belonged to a
planter. The anchor rope was not long, making it useless in any
depth beyond ten feet.

The inlet was wide and seemed to run far inland. To starboard
it widened into a little bay. I steered for the center of that, for
there were some shacks there and a little wooden jetty.

"If there is water enough we can tie up," I shouted to Sam
while pointing to the jetty. He was standing forward on the
halfdeck ready to let go the anchor. There was no other rope
except for the one attached to the anchor, and we would have to
use that for tying her up. As the wind was almost aft, I decided
to take down the mainsail and make our approach under the jib

alone. Neither Sam nor I were true seamen, though both of us had earned our sea legs on board the pirate ships. I had once been allowed to steer the *Queen Anne's Revenge*, but only for a short while. Now, coming up to the little jetty was my first real act of handling a boat. Even without the mainsail, it seemed to me that we were going very fast. I let out the jib sheet, so the sail fluttered in the wind but did not draw the boat.

A black man was sitting on the jetty, a fishing rod in his hand. As we approached he pulled up his line. Just as we came within a few feet of the tiny, wooden structure, our keel struck the bottom. Sam threw the end of the rope to the fisherman, and he tied us up. It was near or just after low tide, and the top of the jetty was far above us. The black man leaned out and asked us something that we did not understand. He repeated it slowly, and I gathered he wanted to know where we came from. I pointed in the general direction of north, hoping that would satisfy him. Once we had taken down the jib, we climbed up the little wooden ladder attached to the end of the jetty.

The fisherman was ancient and toothless, and the dialect he spoke was not familiar. Still, we were able to understand that the place we had landed was called Edisto Island and it was owned by his master. He was so old and useless that no work was asked of him, and he lived in one of the huts we had seen near the jetty.

He invited us to his home, where he had a small vegetable garden and some hens and a little pig. An old crone, nearly as ancient as he, was plucking a chicken. A younger woman, who was their daughter, was there as well. The old man said with pride that she was a house slave, and to prove this asked her to show us her hands. She laughed, and pointing to Sam asked if he was a house slave as well. He held out his hands to her and she nodded with satisfaction. "Do they feed you well?" she asked, surprising us with her English. She had learned it well from her master.

"My master and I are usually well fed, but right now we are terribly hungry. If you would sell us some food we would pay you well. Also, we would like some water, for the water we have on board is not fit to drink."

"He is not your master, you are a runaway." The woman looked Sam straight in the face.

"Runaway," Sam said very slowly. "No...a walkaway...no, a sailaway, maybe." Then he laughed. "I have not run away, but if I had, what would you do?"

The woman turned her gaze to the bay and the sea, then she said, "Nothing. If I turned you in, my master would get the money."

"And if you sell us some food, you will get the money," I said, which made the woman laugh. She turned and spoke to her parents. The old man answered her and his wife held out the plucked chicken.

For one silver and four copper coins from Sam's patrimony, we bought the chicken, some freshly-baked cornbread and best of all, a whole sack of sweet potatoes. We gave them the biscuits to feed to their hens, knowing that they would consider the worms in them a special delicacy.

We got some fruit as well, as it was mid-summer and plentiful. The old woman fried some sowbelly with grits, and Sam and I ate until we could eat no more. There was no decent drinking water, but the old couple's daughter would show us where we could get it. Sam took the keg and followed her, while I stayed by the boat. He was gone a long time, and I was beginning to get nervous when he finally returned.

"I rinsed the keg out several times," he said. "Besides, it was quite far away, almost up by the big house. Were you worried?"

"Yes," I nodded. "I thought she might have decided to tell her master. Let's go. I don't feel safe."

It was nearly high tide, and the boat was level with the jetty. Sam jumped on board and we hoisted both jib and mainsail before we cast off. The wind was still from the northeast. The cutter could sail quite close to the wind, especially after we got the staysail up as well, but it was hard work. We had just cleared the inlet, when I happened to glance into the space under the halfdeck where all the food was stored. I spied the chicken and asked Sam, "I wonder what it will taste like raw?"

He grinned and shook his head and dived in under the half-deck, returning with something in his hand. He held it out for me to see. It was the major's tinderbox.

"More patrimony?" I asked and Sam nodded, and then we both laughed.

All afternoon we sailed southward. The wind was light and I kept as near shore as I dared. In the southern part of the Carolinas there were many deserted beaches where we could land, and they were filled with driftwood that was well dried. When the sun was low in the sky, we saw a beach that looked deserted. It was getting towards low tide, we took down the mainsail and drifted in towards the beach. Fifty yards from shore our keel touched bottom and I put her into the wind. Sam threw the anchor overboard and we took down the foresails.

We raced to shore and Sam was the better swimmer. Then we ran along the beach. It was wonderful to run after having been cooped up so long on board a ship. By the time we collected wood for a fire, the sun was red as blood just above the horizon. We went back to the ship for the chicken and the tinderbox, and managed to get them to shore without soaking them.

Chapter 23

An unwelcome visitor

WHATEVER WAYS THERE ARE TO COOK A chicken in an open fire, neither Sam nor I knew any of them. Finally, we cut it into pieces, stuck the meat on sticks, and held them over the dying fire. Parts were burned and parts were raw, but they tasted good. And the sweet potatoes buried in the sand just underneath the fire came out well. When we had eaten the last of them, we fed the fire some more wood. We certainly did not need it for warmth, but it was nice to look into the flames.

"It is strange, but I can't help feeling sorry for Captain Teach. It isn't that I don't think he deserves whatever punishment he will get if they catch him." With a stick I poked in the dying fire and sparks flew.

"There is only one punishment for piracy—hanging." Sam threw a few more twigs on the fire and it flared up. "My father will end that way, I am sure of that. He will blame it all on his cursed fate and grandfather Peachell. But in truth, he will be hanged because he is a fool." Sam laughed. "That is funny, isn't it?

The punishment for being a fool is hanging. Captain Morgan was probably twice as cruel as my father ever could imagine being, but he wasn't a fool, so he wasn't hanged. He was made a knight by the king instead."

"And governor of Jamaica as well," I added. "That is why I can't help feeling a little sorry for Captain Teach. He is a fine sailor, a clever man, only..." I stopped because I didn't know what else to say.

"Only he is mad," Sam suggested and I nodded because that was true, he was mad. "I think I know why. You see, he was not a real captain, only a pirate one, and they don't count. He had sailed for the king, but before the mast. He had probably been ordered about by officers not half as clever as he, but they wore a cocked hat and he didn't."

"And he wanted to wear one as well?" I asked

"Why not?" Sam pointed to the rising moon. "Don't you think a clever slave would want to be a master?" The last words were spoken low.

"You are not a slave, Sam." Without thinking about it I, too, had lowered my voice almost to a whisper.

"Yes, I am." Sam smiled. "I am like the moon that rises and sets. Forget about it, Will. What I try not to be is a slave inside myself. My body is a slave to the major, but that does not mean that my spirit cannot be free."

"Major Bonnet is on the *Revenge*, he is not here," I pointed out.

"But maybe he is here!" Sam slapped his chest. "Maybe he is here!"

I poked the fire again with my stick, baring the embers that hid beneath the white ashes. "When we get to Jamaica, you will be free. I am sure my father..."

Sam made an irritated gesture with his hand. "Your father can't set me free, only I can do that."

I desperately wanted Sam to be happy because he was my friend, the first real friend I had ever had. "You are cleverer than I am. It was you who took the money and the tinderbox. I had not even thought of it," I admitted.

"In some places they brand slaves like they would an animal. You know why? Because they know that the hot iron burns not only the skin but the slave's heart and brain as well. I will say that for my father—none of his slaves were branded."

I did not know if my father's were. The plantation was inland. I had been there once only, but I had seen the slaves, and some of them had been laughing.

"Do you remember John Husk?" I asked.

"The wind blows free across the sea, And brothers we will be." Sam sang the last lines from the young pirate's song. I had never heard him sing before, and he had a good voice. I could never carry a tune.

"Why did he become a pirate?" I asked.

"How should I know?" Sam stretched himself and yawned.

"I liked him. He was the only one of the pirates I liked," I said, stretching out on the sand a little away from the fire.

"I didn't dislike him, he did me no harm. But he was a fool, and I would not trust him, either," Sam murmured.

The moon had set, the cloud-free sky was starfilled. I closed my eyes, locking out the world, and soon I was asleep.

It was not the rising sun just peeking above the horizon that woke me, but a sharp kick in my side. I looked up into the grinning face of a man with a black beard and shaggy hair. For a moment, as I was still half asleep, I thought it was Captain Teach, but then I realized that this man was much younger. I turned to look for Sam, but he was not there. Our little cutter was riding free, the tide was high.

"A little runaway. You didn't like the cut of your master's jib, and so you stole a boat and ran away."

"I am no runaway," I said furiously and sat up. "And I have no master." By his language I realized that the man was a sailor, ship-wrecked or sent ashore by his captain.

"But you have a nice boat. I like her lines, she will suit me nicely." The sailor spat on the sand. "Two days I have been stranded here. The beach stretched on a mile or two in that direction, then there is open water. Inland is nothing but swamp." The sailor pointed south and then west. "I would take you along, but I am not fond of company."

"You are a castaway, put ashore from some ship," I screamed furiously, while I crawled away like a crab.

"There was some slight disagreement between me and a certain Captain Vane," the sailor admitted, grinning.

"You are a pirate," I said, standing up and ready to run.

"Pirate is what those call us who are always chasing us with a noose. I prefer lord of the ocean, or gentleman of the sea. How did you know I belonged among them?"

"Captain Teach talked about Captain Vane. He once said that if he got hanged first, then he would meet him in hell."

"So you have sailed with Blackbeard. A bit too young for the profession, I wager." The pirate turned towards the sea and I rushed at him, but he threw me aside with ease, and as I fell on the sand, he gave me a kick. "Little fool," he said, and waded out into the sea.

I did not even get up. I just lay where I had fallen and watched the pirate make his way out to our little cutter. Near the boat, the water was up to his shoulders. He reached for the gunwale and pulled himself up. When he was about to get one knee up on the deck, a figure in the cockpit rose and hit him a sharp blow on the head. Before he fell back in the water he received yet another blow. Then Sam shouted, "Come aboard."

I rushed down into the sea, keeping on the sea side of the cutter. Sam gave me a hand and pulled me up into the boat. "Where is he?" I spluttered. In my haste I had swallowed some water.

"Out there getting a weapon." Sam grinned and pointed to the pirate who was searching for a stick stout enough to fight with. "We better hoist sail. I have a feeling he would prove a difficult passenger."

We did not bother to hoist more than the staysail and jib. The pirate had found himself a pole as tall as himself, and was wading out to do battle. Sam was ready to pull out the tiller, for that was the weapon he had used before. The tide was still coming in, and as I pulled on the anchor tow, the cutter floated farther out to sea. The pirate stopped when the water reached his shoulders. The wind was light but from the southwest. When we had hoisted the mainsail, the castaway pirate was just a tiny figure standing forlornly on the beach.

"How did you know he was there?" I asked as we headed out into the open sea.

"I didn't." Sam shook his head. "But when we were gathering wood in the evening, I noticed some footprints in the sand that seemed fresh. It bothered me enough to wake me in the middle of the night. I decided to go on board but I left you to sleep, for I wasn't sure if I had just imagined it."

"He was a pirate, belonged to Captain Vane's ship." I looked back, the beach seemed empty now.

"I wish I had killed him, then." Sam, too, looked back towards land. "Vane was even crueller than Blackbeard."

"He didn't want to be called pirate. Lord of the ocean, he pre-ferred," I said, laughing.

"Lord castaway will do for him. I don't think he could swim. Did he hurt you?"

"Twice he kicked me, and I can still feel it. But I will be all right." I noticed that the sea had become a deeper blue. I pulled the sheets as tight as I could, and changed the course as near to south as the boat would head. "I owe you my life," I said.

Sam shrugged then smiled. "I saved my own life, too. I had no wish to be marooned on that beach."

Chapter 24

The Indian family

WE CONTINUED TO SAIL SOUTH, KEEPING THE coast a low, blue line west of us. The wind was favorable but very light. Soon we had eaten the last of our food, except for some uncooked sweet potatoes. Four days after we had escaped from the castaway pirate, Sam was so hungry that he tried to eat a raw sweet potato, but in spite of his hunger he couldn't swallow it.

"Let's try to land and see if we can buy some food," I suggested. "We must be out of the Carolinas by now. I think we are in Florida and that is ruled by Spain. At least, they speak Spanish there. Do you know the language?"

"Buenos dias," Sam grinned and asked if that would do.

"A little more than 'good day' is probably necessary. Do you know anything else?" I asked.

"'Quanto' means 'How much.'" Sam looked towards the coast where we were now heading. "I wonder," he said, "if they will take our money? The gold coin, yes, but maybe the silver will be all right, too. What about you, do you speak any Spanish?"

121

"My father had me learn Latin for a while, but my teacher was a drunk and he fired him. But I do know some words. If we get food and water, we can head for the Bahamas. They should be that way," I pointed over my shoulder to the sea.

"The land is very low and flat." Sam was looking ahead. "I hope we don't run aground too far out."

"The moon was but a sickle last night, so it must be near to neap tide." Suddenly I realized that I was acting the captain, in spite of my knowing no more about seamanship than Sam.

"Do you want to steer?" I asked.

"You take her in, then I can laugh when you put her aground." Sam jumped up on the halfdeck and peered down into the ocean. "There is plenty of water yet, and a fine sandy bottom. When we anchor up I am going for a good swim."

"The wind is dying. We won't reach land much before sunset." The staysail was flapping idly, and I thought if the tide was going out we wouldn't make it at all.

The sun was just setting when Sam cast the anchor. It was low tide but we still had a foot or so of water under the keel. The beach seemed to stretch forever, and there were no houses to be seen. We swam to shore and took a run along the sand. Funny, I thought, we had not eaten well on the pirate ship or on our own, either. Yet I never felt so well as I do now. I looked at Sam. Both of us were thin but strong.

Suddenly, Sam stopped running and pointed to a spot ahead of us. A thin column of smoke was rising from a point a little inland. "You go back to the boat, but collect wood for a fire on the way. I will try and see what we can get from there." Sam nodded in the direction of the smoke.

"But we didn't bring the money." I said.

"You didn't," Sam grinned, "but I did." He took out a silver coin, threw it high in the air, and caught it on its way down.

I walked back to the boat, picking up pieces of wood along the way. Then I swam out to the boat. I got the tinderbox, and let myself gently back down into the water. It reached to my shoulder, so I could wade ashore holding the tinderbox above my head.

When I got the fire going and Sam had not yet shown up, I returned to the boat for our water keg and some sweet potatoes. I took the two wine bottles as well, to fill with water, for the water in the keg still had an unpleasant flavor. Getting everything to shore would be tricky. The sea was now almost up to my neck. The keg could float beside me, but I didn't want the yams to get wet. I managed to get where the water was lower, pushing the keg in front with my chest and holding the bottles and yams high in the air. On shore, I drank some water, and washed my face in the rest of the water left in the keg. Then I sat down and waited for Sam, as the fire was burning too well to roast the potatoes, yet.

Soon we would have to head out into the open sea. The sun rose in the east and set in the west, so at least twice a day I would know my directions. On a chart I had seen on the *Queen Anne's Revenge*, there were many islands that stretched roughly south. If I followed them we should eventually get to the island of Hispaniola, and from there Jamaica was at the most one or two day's sail.

Sam was finally coming, carrying a basket slung from his shoulder. It seemed heavy and promised a good supper. I could not wait to see what it contained and ran to meet him. Sam put down the basket and took from it a piece of bread, real bread like I used to get at home and thought nothing of. I grabbed it and stuffed it into my mouth. Sam watched me, grinning while I ate it. "There is more," he said, "so we shall eat well tonight."

"It is funny. I had almost forgotten what bread tastes like." We had returned to the fire and I was looking through the basket. There was only half a loaf, but it was a lot better than no bread at all. I picked up some meat that looked very strange, and asked

Sam what it was. He grinned and said it was alligator tail. I dropped the piece back into the basket. There were two fish as well, and a lot of fruit.

"Go and get some water," Sam ordered. "I will start cooking meat."

"Aye, aye, sir," I said and saluted. I took the keg and the two bottles and headed in the direction of the thin spiral of smoke still visible in the darkening evening air.

A fire was burning in front of a hut made of branches and thatched with reeds. An old crone sat at the fire, languidly stirring a pot. I held out the little keg and said "water" in Spanish. The old lady nodded and shouted a name. A boy about my own age, completely naked, came from inside their home, and the woman spoke to him in a language I did not understand.

He reached out to take the little barrel, and I gave him the bottles as well. He ran off and disappeared among the bushes that surrounded their settlement. I squatted by the fire near the old lady, and she smiled. She had no teeth, and her face looked as if it had been carved in wood. I realized that these were Indians. There had been Indians, too, in Jamaica but they had died out, or most likely been killed.

From the little hut came three younger children, two girls and a boy. They squatted across from me and stared at me silently. Their mother, still young, came as well, and asked something of the old lady. I could not understand the answer, but it made the children laugh. I joined in the merriment, and made the children laugh even more.

The boy returned with the water, and indicated I should take the two bottles. I wanted to take the keg as well, but he shook his head and pointed in the direction of the beach. As first I was afraid that he wanted to keep our keg, but he merely wanted to carry it.

I could smell the alligator meat frying as we came near our fire. Sam had made skewers from driftwood, and was busy trying to

keep the food from burning instead of cooking. He did not suc-
ceed with all of it. Some of the meat was charred, but tasted even
better because of it. The two fish were fine, and even though the
skin was blackened, they were delicious.

The Indian boy sat across from us, watching intently while
we ate. Sam offered him some alligator meat, but he shook his
head. Twice he said something we could not understand, and
then it was our turn to shake our heads. There were so many
questions I wanted to ask the boy, but he seemed to know only
a few words in Spanish and no English at all.

Sam, who was eager to acquire some fishing tackle, finally made
him understand the connection between the copper coin he held
in his hand, and the dumb show he had acted out to describe the
line and hook. Finally the boy nodded and disappeared in the
darkness. A little while later he reappeared with a line with two
hooks attached to it. Sam handed him the coin. The boy examined
it, and then to our surprise stuck it into his mouth as he left.

"But where else could he have put it," Sam said staring into
the darkness, and that was true since the boy had been completely naked. This made us both laugh, though we were not
overly dressed ourselves. The moon rose, a sickle in the sky. We
roasted more sweet potatoes to keep as provisions for the next
few days, and we still had some bread left. I wondered where the
bread had come from, and if the Indians could have baked it.

Maybe there was a village nearby. That thought made me sug-
gest that we sleep on board. I had no wish to be awakened as I
had been by the pirate when last we slept on the beach.

At low tide we covered the embers of the fire with sand and
waded out to our boat carrying all our possessions. As I lay
down to sleep, I suddenly realized that if our little boat had a
name I didn't know it. I suggested to Sam that we should name
it, in the tradition of all boats.

"William's Folly," Sam grunted, already half asleep.

Chapter 25

We find the islands

THE WIND WAS FAIR WHEN WE WOKE IN THE morning, the tide just turning, and all was well. We took our time getting ready, but finally we could not think of any good reason for prolonging our departure.

"The islands must be just east of here, no more than a day's sail at most. If we have not sighted one by morning, then we shall change course," I said as we got underway.

"I think the ocean is very big." Sam looked ahead out to sea and then added, "And our boat is very small."

"It will feel even smaller when we are out of sight of land and more like a nutshell if it starts to blow," I said and glanced back. Already the coast seemed far away. The bushes that had been distinct before were now just greenery in the distance.

"Faith in the captain is very important, I believe," Sam grunted. "But if my foolish father could find his way around this watery world, I see no reason why you should not be able to."

126

"The confidence of the crew is appreciated. I just wish that I had as much faith in the captain as you have," I said laughing. "I saw a chart of the islands in the cabin of the *Queen Anne's Revenge*. There were a lot of them, so I don't think we can miss them all."

"If we do, then we just change course," Sam mocked and grinning, added, "that is, if we can figure out the difference between south and north."

"South is that way," I said and pointed in the direction that I thought was south. "So long as I can see land, I know the difference."

"What about when night has come and the land has gone?" Sam asked.

I had been thinking about that myself as I did not know the stars. "If the wind remains steady, I should be able to hold this course even though it has grown dark. But if the wind changes, it might be best to take down the sails and just drift until the sun tells us where east is."

"Fair enough, captain." Sam climbed up on the halfdeck and seated himself. "I dreamt last night of my father. It is strange. He haunts me in my sleep as he used to do when I was awake. Shall I ever escape him?"

"Do you really want to?" I asked, looking back towards land. The shore was still visible enough but only as a thin line. If the land had not been so flat, we might have kept sight of it until reaching the islands.

"I suppose something within me does not." Sam wrinkled his brow in thought. "Maybe it is the blood calling. He is my father after all. In my dream he was wretched, in some kind of prison. Do you dream of your father?"

I shook my head. "Not very often. More often of Mary and sometimes even of my mother. But I have dreamt of Captain Teach several times."

"Blackbeard!" Sam scowled. "I have no use for him. Good men can do evil, but men as evil as Captain Teach seldom do good. He is the kind of man that one knows by instinct to stay away from."

"He did not harm me," I protested.

"He plundered your father's ship and took you prisoner. Is that not harming you?"

"That is true," I agreed unhappily, "but he didn't do anything to me."

"What you mean is that he didn't give you a back like mine, or put you in chains or keelhaul you. I wouldn't be too grateful for that. He would have done it if he felt like it. He just didn't." Sam yawned as the heat of the midday sun made him sleepy.

"Oh, you are right," I laughed. "I will tell myself to stop dreaming about him."

"Blackbeard could murder a man in the morning and forget that he had done it before the sun set. My father did evil, to me and to others, but at least he suffered because of it. He would cry and curse his grandfather who had caused it all. He would whip me and then ask my forgiveness for having done it. Once he got down on his knees in front of me and asked me to beat him."

"Did you?" I asked, surprised.

"No." Sam smiled and looked away. "Firstly because he wanted me to, and secondly because there was no point to it. I had no wish to become like him, and I told him so. That made him so angry that he almost beat me again, there and then."

I thought Sam cleverer than I, and at times it annoyed me for I liked being clever. But he was also more complex, nothing was simple to him. "I think I would have beaten him if I had been you," I said, for in some ways I disliked the major more than I did Blackbeard.

"I would have killed Blackbeard, and thought I had done a good deed," Sam laughed. "That is if I had gotten a chance to do it. But my father is something else. There were times when I dreamt of killing him, but I don't think I ever would have done it. Strangely enough, when I didn't hate him I felt sorry for him...Oh, look!" Sam pointed to a large school of flying fish which had just emerged from the sea, the sun reflecting on their colored scales. It was a wonderful sight..

As the sun set, the wind became weak and unsteady. We had lost sight of the coast of Florida. The sea was only light blue, which meant that we had not sailed into the deeper ocean, but were either near enough to the coast or on the Bahama Banks. Around the islands I knew there would be no great depth until we came to the islands of Hispaniola and Cuba, and they were far, far away. Just after the sun finally sank beneath the horizon, the wind died completely.

"Let's take the sails down," I suggested, as the boat no longer obeyed its rudder. I let go the tiller and helped Sam, and just as we were finished a large gull perched itself on the masthead.

"That brings luck," Sam declared. "It will keep watch over us while we sleep."

"Is that true?" I asked foolishly, which made Sam laugh.

"If you believe it, then it is true," he declared.

"But I don't." I said, a little annoyed at having been so simple. Just at that moment the gull spread its wings and flew away.

"It heard you." Sam shook his head in mock concern. "But never mind, let's eat."

"If someone believes something that I don't believe, is it then true or not true?" I bit into one of the yams that we had roasted in the fire.

"It is not true to you but true to the one who believes in it." Sam spat out some of the skin that had gotten too charcoaled. "My father believed in slavery, and he could prove it was a good and true arrangement. He said that the Greeks used slaves, and that everyone who was not a fool knew that the Greeks were the most enlightened people in the world."

I disagreed, not about the Greeks, for I knew nothing about them, but about slavery. But to my father, is it not a good and true arrangement, I thought?

"There are lots of things my father and I agreed on. Such as there are stars in the sky at night." Sam glanced up at the starfilled heavens. "We also agreed that the ocean is wet, which means there were at least two things that were true to both of us."

I laughed and so did Sam, then he took my knife and cut two slices of the bread. Handing me one, he declared that it was the end of our supper. I made it last as long as I could and drank a little water, then I lay down to sleep.

Sleep did not come easily, and each time I dozed off, I would wake up again. Near me I could hear Sam sleeping peacefully, and I almost felt like waking him. Just before sunrise I finally fell into a sound sleep, but just as the sun rose, a gull woke me. It circled above the boat, screaming as if it had some important message for me. I got up and looked out over the sea. There was nothing to be seen except for the tip of the sun, visible on the eastern horizon. A light breeze was blowing from the west. I woke Sam and we got the sail up and under way.

"Are you sure that is south?" he asked and pointed ahead.

"Yes, because the sun is telling us where east is. The waters are still not very deep, which means we are not far out in the ocean." We were sailing close haul and I pulled in a little on the mainsheet.

"As far as I am concerned, we are far out enough." Sam shaded his eyes, looking west towards Florida.

"Should we not eat the last of the bread?" I asked. Sam took out what was left of the little loaf and cut it in half, then he handed a piece to me, saying, "breakfast is served, sir."

I thanked him and stared out over the empty sea ahead of us. If my course was correct we should soon see an island.

It was Sam who spotted it, and it was not an island but a group of rocks low in the water. I got so excited at seeing them that I almost let go of the tiller. "It is the beginning of the banks," I shouted.

"I hope the next island will be a little bigger," Sam said as we passed the rocks well to port.

"Oh, there are lots of islands, many of them uninhabited." I looked back at the rocks and then ahead, hoping to see one of the islands, but I didn't.

"I know. Blackbeard is supposed to have buried a treasure on one of them, or so my father told me." Sam smiled. "I wouldn't mind having a sackful of doubloons when we arrive in Jamaica."

"It is blood money. Stolen, all of it," I said with disgust.

"The wonderful thing about gold is that dirt does not stick to it. Whether it has been earned by robbery," Sam paused for a moment, "or by selling people, or by honest work, it shines equally bright."

By late afternoon we had sighted our first island. It was fairly large, but very low, and I was sure that it was not fit to land on. A few hours before sunset we came across another island, smaller, but with a sandy beach. We anchored up and waded ashore. Sam had caught a fish, and we lit a fire and roasted it along with the last of the sweet potatoes.

Sam wanted us to sleep on the beach, where we would have been more comfortable, but I was afraid that our makeshift anchor would not hold. The thought of waking up in the morning and finding our boat gone made me insist on sleeping aboard. In my dreams, I sailed our little boat into the harbour of Port Royal, where my father waited for me on the pier.

Chapter 26

The storm

I WOKE IN THE MORNING TO AN EERIE STILLNESS. No birds were screeching and the air felt heavy, gloomy, and strange. The sea was a dark mirror, and the risen sun obscured by a mist. The island was low and treeless, giving little protection should the wind start to blow. "In bad weather, head for the open sea," I recalled Captain O'Rourke telling me. Well, we could not do that, but maybe we could find an island to hide behind.

"What is wrong?" Sam asked, just waking.

"I don't know, but something is. Can't you feel it?"

"I think a storm is coming up, a hurricane maybe."

Sam breathed deeply as if he wanted to taste the air. Then looking with scorn at the island he said, "This won't be much of a shelter."

"As soon as a bit of wind comes, let's head for that island." I pointed to an island in the distance to the east. It was higher and tree covered. In lee of that we might be able to shelter, though I did not think our anchor would hold. Suddenly a bit of wind came, and we quickly set the staysail and mainsail and pulled up anchor. We had the wind almost aft, but it was not steady and shifted all the time. Still, we made quick headway, and we were more than halfway to the island when the wind suddenly died as quickly as it had sprung up.

"What now?" I asked as the boom of the mainsail swung back and forth.

"Now nothing, but soon something." Sam pointed towards the east, where the sky had turned an ominous black. "What about taking down the sails, captain?"

We had just furled and made safe the mainsail when the wind hit us. With only the staysail up, our little boat was forging through the waters. Whitecaps sprung up everywhere as the wind whipped the sea. I only hoped the staysail would hold, and wished we had put up the much smaller jib. The wind was now from the northeast, steady and ferocious.

I could still hold the course for the island, but what if the stay-sail ripped? I let out the sheet of the staysail a little, trying to ease the pressure on it. But that did not help for it bulged. And then with a loud bang it split and the wind tore it into ribbons. Now there was no chance of reaching the island. We could not put up the jib, and even if we could have, it probably would have torn as we hoisted it.

I changed course, letting the wind on hull and mast decide where we were going to end up. Driven by the storm in a southwestern direction, I feared that sooner or later an island or worse, possibly a reef or some rocks, would bar our way. The shallow water on the banks made the waves very short and caused them to break almost as soon as they were formed. The sea was a mass of white foam, and any reef or stones would not be visible in the boiling fury of the breaking waters.

"Will we be all right?" Sam shouted in my ear. The noise of the hurricane making it almost impossible to hear.

"No!" I shouted back, laughing at the same time, for I suddenly felt mysteriously lighthearted.

"Good," Sam laughed as well. "I was afraid we might live."

I could steer a little, so if I spied an island far enough ahead I might be able to miss it. But suddenly the wind dropped and God opened up a waterfall from the skies. It was not rain, but a mass of water that suddenly descended on us.

"We are in the eye of the storm," Sam yelled. He needn't have, for now a sullen stillness was even more frightening. "It will come in the other direction now," he said quietly.

The wind had pressed the boat in one direction, and now the waves played with it, making it swing around and roll and toss like the little nutshell it was. I suddenly felt ill, and Sam did not look well either. There was nothing I could do, for without the wind I had no steerage. Still, I held on to the tiller.

The wind came back, as Sam had predicted, in the opposite direction, as suddenly as it had ceased. It seemed to me even stronger than before. Now we returned more or less in the same direction we had come from. If we could traverse the same waters, we would be all right, unless I hit a rock. Suddenly ahead in the water, we saw a whole palm tree. We missed it, but soon I spotted other debris, parts of the roof of a house, I thought, or was it a wall. Then the overturned jollyboat of some ship. I pointed to it, wondering if some unlucky person had been on board. Swimming in that foaming sea would be impossible.

At last the wind lessened and the sun appeared. The hurricane had passed. Sam and I looked at each other. "We are alive," I said and grabbed both his hands. For a while we stood like that, then at the same moment we both shouted as loud as we could, "We are alive!" I shall always remember that moment as long as I live.

A shallow sea is quickly whipped into a turmoil by the winds, and for the same reason it soon returns to calmness once the storm is over. By evening there were no more whitecaps showing, and the only sign of the hurricane was the debris floating in the water. The sunset was more glorious than usual, maybe because of the storm.

The sky turned so very red in the west it seemed to have caught fire from the setting sun. The wind was now light and we decided that it was best to take down sails and anchor up for the night. I could see no islands near, but the depth of the sea was still shallow enough that we could use our anchor. The bottom seemed to be sandy, and if the anchor did not hold us at least it would prevent us from drifting too far. I wished we had some more rope, for the longer the anchor tow, the safer is your ship.

"Did you see the jollyboat?" I asked as we sat and ate what was left of our provisions.

"Yes," Sam nodded. "I saw something else as well. Maybe the two belonged together."

"What was it?" I asked, already half-guessing the answer from the expression on Sam's face.

"It was just after we passed the jollyboat. A sailor, I think. His face was turned towards me and for a moment I thought he was staring at me, then he disappeared."

"Was he dead?"

"Oh, yes. No one could survive in that sea." Sam shivered as if he was cold. "I thought then that I was going to join him soon. I wonder who he was? His face was almost blue. Let's talk of something else. About food. Roasted chickens for instance. What is your favorite?"

"Suckling pig, well roasted, though it is kind of horrid to eat something so young."

"The skin all crisp—yes, I like that, too, and a roasted duck is not bad, either. Why does anyone want to become a sailor? You starve most of the time and scared some of the time, and sick and uncomfortable all the time."

"I don't know," I said. "You might even end up like the drowned man you saw, yet I don't know." I smiled. "I think I would like to become a sailor."

"Captain, you mean." Sam smiled. "I wouldn't even care for that. No, if you ever get us to Jamaica, I shall jump ashore and never tread the planks of a deck again. Do you know what I dreamt about every night I spent on board a ship? Food! What about a big dish of fried squid?" Sam lay down on the floor of the cockpit. "Tonight I am going to dream about that," he announced, and closed his eyes.

When I woke in the morning the sea was so calm that I could look down and see our anchor. We had not drifted at all. We were very hungry, we had no food left, and Sam had nothing he could use as bait. Swimming only made us hungrier, though it did make us cleaner as well.

As the sun rose a breeze sprung up and we got under way. We had lost our staysail which was particularly useful in light winds. I steered for an island south of us that had some trees on it. I hoped it was not deserted and that we might be able to buy food.

As we came nearer, I saw something sticking up above the trees on the other side of the island. "It is a mast," Sam declared and I nodded in agreement. But if it was a mast it was at a strange angle.

"A shipwreck?" Sam asked.

"I think so. I can't see anyone ashore, can you?"

"No, but we better be careful. If they have lost their ship, they may be a little too eager to get another."

"Yes," I agreed. "I will sail around the island, and you keep a watch."

We could see nothing alive on the island, but when we rounded it we got a clear view of the wreck. It was a schooner, its foremast snapped midway, the mainmast pointing to the sky, bits of canvas still hanging to the topsailspar. Two guns that had broken loose lay upside down against the bulwark, and she was well up upon the beach. I looked at Sam and he at me, and we both said, "Pirate."

Chapter 27

What the pirate ship hid

AFTER WE HAD ANCHORED, WE WAITED FOR A
while before we dared go ashore. We did not tie the sail but left
it to be hoisted at a moment's notice. But as nothing stirred on
the island we finally swam ashore.

"We shall at least be able to get some rope, and maybe a better anchor and anchor tow as well," I said as Sam and I got onto
the beach. Both of us were as naked as the Indian boy we had met
in Florida.

"I wonder if there if food on board." Sam contemplated the
wreck. It was a vessel of a couple of hundred tons. She was
lying in the shallows near the shore, her keel firmly embedded
in the sand. So much rigging was hanging from the mast still
standing, that it was easy to find a rope to help us climb
onboard. She had been schooner-rigged but with two square
topsails as well. She had been fast, I thought, a virtue a pirate
ship needs. She was lying at an angle, but we could still walk
its deck. Its bulwalk had been broken in one place and I thought

the rest of the guns on board must have disappeared through that gap.

"She must have had much too much canvas up when the storm hit her," Sam grunted.

"She probably went right over," I agreed. "Whoever was on deck ended up in the sea."

"Let's go below." Sam nodded towards the hatch to the fore-castle. The hatchcover was open. The quarters below were in a sad state. The schooner must have hit a rock before she was beached, for two planks had been stowed in, and the sea was vis-ible through the opening. When the tide rose, it would be flooded. Clothes and hammocks were lying everywhere, covered by a layer of sand. Sam picked up a flintlock pistol, a very pretty weapon that would fetch a good price in Kingston.

The galley was in the center of what had been the crew's quarters. I spied some tin plates among the rubbish, and thought I would take them later.

A door leading to a passage aft had swung open, and beyond were the captain's and the master's cabins. I noticed that the door could be bolted on the captain's side, a very wise precau-tion, for the crew of a pirate ship is not very trustworthy. Many a pirate captain has ended up with his throat slit in the night.

The floors of the cabins here were higher than in the forepart of the ship, and only water had entered. Sam went straight for a door aft, turning as he opened it.

"This is where the weapons are kept, the best wine and rum, and most important of all, bread, if there is any on board." There were: eight loaves and two sacks of flour; some bottles of wine as well; and a whole armory of small arms and dirks and cutlasses. Sam picked up a dirk and tried to cut the bread. It was almost as hard as stone, but by putting it down on the deck he managed to cut off two chunks. I tried to take a bite, but found it too hard. "We will soak it in water and then it will be fine," Sam said.

The captain's cabin was on the port side. Sam knocked on the door. We waited a moment, half expecting someone to say "come in," but all was silent. The cabin was not large, but some efforts had been made to make it comfortable. A desk was bolted to the floor but its drawers and their contents were all over the place. Among the mess I spied a chart, and eagerly picked it up. I could make out the islands of Cuba and Hispaniola and below them, Jamaica.

A dim glow came from the skylight. The door of a closet containing the captain's clothes swung to and fro. A fine sword still in its scabbard hung from the door. I took it down. Its sheath was still attached to its belt, so I put it on. I must have been a very comical sight for I was otherwise completely naked. It made Sam laugh but he soon stopped. We both heard something moving.

The sound came from the berth, which we had not bothered to look at before because it was in the shadow of the deck above us. In a corner of the berth was something black, the pirate flag, with the picture of a white skull grinning up at us. But something else was under it, something alive, small, maybe a dog, I thought, as I whipped the pirate banner away.

A girl, about ten or twelve years old, was crouched almost into a ball, with her face against the hull of the ship. I looked at Sam, his face was screwed up in surprise. I quickly undid the sword and wrapped the pirate flag around me, and Sam ran to the captain's closet to find something to cover his nakedness.

"We won't do you any harm," I said, and touched the girl's shoulder gently. She did not answer but pressed herself even tighter against the planks of the shipside. "We are not pirates," I mumbled.

"Here." Sam threw me a pair of kneebreeches, which I hurriedly put on. They were too large but not by much. The pirate captain must have been a small man. Sam had wrapped a scarf around himself and looked decent enough for female company. "Tell her our names and that we are but boys still," he suggested.

"My name is William," I paused, "William Bernard. I was a captive of the pirate, Blackbeard. I come from Jamaica." At the word Jamaica the girl turned to look at me, and she nodded as if she understood what I had said. "We will not harm you, but help you. Were you a captive, here?"

The girl did not answer, only nodded once more. "Are you from Jamaica?" I asked.

"Yes," she whispered and sat up.

Her hair was a mass of dark curls and her eyes big and black. She was of Spanish blood, probably from one of the old families of the island.

"What is your name?" I asked.

"Constanza," she whispered, but on seeing Sam she backed up in a corner of the berth.

"This is Sam Bonnet. He is a friend of mine and was captured by the pirates, too." Sam smiled and held out his open hands to show he was no longer carrying the pistol.

"We have a little boat we are sailing back to Jamaica. We will take you along." I don't know if it was Sam's words or his smile, but the girl seemed less frightened.

"They went away," she said as if telling me a secret. "The wind started to blow something terrible. He ran up on deck and never came down again. So I hid in his berth."

"That was very clever of you. How old are you?" I asked.

"Come Christmas, I will be twelve. How old are you?" she asked still staring at Sam, not me.

"Fourteen." And then I suddenly realized that I might actually be fifteen, for my birthday was in September and surely we had reached that month.

"I am sixteen, and I come from Barbados." Sam turned to me.

"Let's go above. We must take from this ship what we need before it is observed, and someone comes to plunder it."

"Come," I said to the girl. For a moment I did not think she would obey me. The dress she wore had once been of good quality, but now it was in rags and her feet were bare. As we left, I spotted the sword and picked it up. I wanted very much to keep it.

We kept watch while we took from the pirate ship whatever we thought worthwhile. The bread was edible if soaked in water. We made a bed for the girl under the halfdeck in our boat, and told her to stay there. She was oddly obedient, her big eyes shifting from me to Sam, but all the time mute. All we had learned from her so far was that she came from my island, and that she had been on board a ship captured by pirates.

We waited almost too long in plundering the pirate ship. Maybe we had become too greedy. We did not take any weapons beyond my sword and the pistol Sam had picked up, and a small dirk each. Sam did not bother to get powder for his weapon. I got plenty of rope and some more iron to add to our anchor. Sam went through the captain's cabin looking for money, and he found a purse with a few gold coins. Our greatest find, and it was I who made it, was a small hand compass which I discovered in the master's cabin. Now I would always know where south was.

I had just returned on deck dragging up a spare jib that I thought I could make into a staysail, when I saw a boat steering for our island. I called Sam who was below.

She was cutter-rigged as well, but I guessed a little smaller than ours. When Sam saw her, he said nothing, but immediately jumped from the schooner into the water and headed for our little boat. I followed him, still keeping the schooner's jib. The tide had come in and was now more than waist deep by our boat. I handed the jib to Sam who was already on board, and he gave me a hand as I scrambled up. It took us no time at all to set the sails and pull up the anchor. The breeze was light, blowing from the northwest. I let the sails out and steered southeast.

As we got free of the island, we got a better view of the company coming. I did not know if they were pirates, but of one thing I was certain: that if they had managed to surprise us, we would have lost everything we had, probably including our lives.

When they saw us they changed their course, trying to catch us. But their boat was heavily manned, and they soon realized that ours was the faster one. A couple of musket shots were fired after us, but they did us no harm. At the sound of shots Constanza came up. She looked at the other boat and uttered two words: "Pirates," and then, "Men."

I laughed, but seeing the fear in her face, I mumbled I was sorry and tried to comfort her by saying that there was no danger. It was true. By now, the other boat had gone about, and headed for the island and the stranded pirate schooner.

"I wish I knew why she was so frightened," I whispered foolishly to Sam. The girl had returned to her place under the halfdeck.

Sam raised an eyebrow quizzically. "You don't know?" he asked, and I shook my head even though I suspected that I did know. "Once," Sam kept his voice low, "on my father's ship the men took a woman on board from a prize they had taken. My father was against it, but for all his being captain he was hardly in command." Sam glanced for a moment towards the girl and then lowered his voice even more. "She begged for mercy, but got none, and during the night she managed to jump into the sea and drown herself."

I did not know what to say. I pulled in on the sheet a little and straightened our course directly south.

Chapter 28

The Waterspout

AMONG THE PLUNDER FROM THE SHIP WERE some splendid clothes, which fitted us badly. It would have been better if I had remembered to take the chart that I had seen in the captain's cabin, even though most charts are not accurate enough to be of great value. In my mind I had a picture of the position of the islands, and that would have to be enough. But the little compass was a true godsend. I felt sure that as long as I steered south I could not possibly miss Cuba or Hispaniola. If I first made a landfall on either of them, then I could easily set a course for Jamaica.

Wounds of the flesh heal. True, they may leave a scar, but eventually even the pain and the fear you felt when you received them is forgotten. But injuries to your soul may leave wounds that never heal, festering sores that spring up and bleed years afterward. Such were the hurts that Constanza had suffered. Fear never left the depth of her eyes, and we often heard her weeping in her sleep.

Sam talked to her, and once I heard him tell her the story of his own miserable life. Strangely enough, it was exactly that story that seemed to help her. His suffering somehow made hers easier to bear, and she was at last able to talk about what had happened. There had been a great slaughter on board her ship. Most of the men had been cut down, among them her father. Her mother and a maid had been spared, as had a few of the sailors. The rigging had been cut, leaving them only two sails to make port with. This was done to prevent them from raising the alarm while the pirates were still in the vicinity.

"I saw my mother. She stood by the railing of the ship and held out her hands to me. I wanted to jump into the sea, too, but I did not know how to swim, and I was scared that a shark might eat me. I wish I had jumped and that a shark had eaten me."

"But you are alive! That is better than being eaten by a shark," I said, sitting at the tiller. It was the third day after we had found her in the shipwrecked pirate ship.

"Yes, I'm alive, but I'm not the Constanza my mother knew ..." The girl looked at Sam. "Sometimes when I think I am, I remember the men and what they did."

"One can never go back, all roads lead ahead." Sam smiled for a moment. "But that is good, too, because that means there is hope. The pirates are gone, and they are probably all dead."

"No, they are not!" Constanza said angrily. "Last night when I was asleep they all came back, and did ..." her voice became a whisper, "what they did before."

"I used to feel the pain of the whip on my back, when no one was touching me, and the anger and the fear. But lately I have not felt it. I sleep and dream, but in my dreams no one hurts me."

Constanza shook her head as if she did not believe it, but at the same time looked with such fondness at Sam that I think she was grateful for what he had said.

Clouds had covered the sun. I felt the weather was changing and it might become dirty. We took a reef in our mainsail, the wind had become a little stronger, and suddenly I saw ahead a strange sight—a big, black cloud with a long tube of equal darkness running down into the sea. It was about a mile ahead of us on our course.

"Look," I shouted, pointing to it.

"A water spout," Sam said, "I have seen one before on the *Revenge*. It is a very strong wind that sucks up water, and swirls round and round at such speed that it can rip your sails to pieces in a moment. Steer clear of it."

I changed course a little. The strange spout of water and wind that emerged from the cloud did not move fast over the sea. At a very sedate speed it came toward us, and seemed to me not dangerous at all. "It will pass well to starboard," I said to Sam who was watching it as fascinated as I was.

As we came nearer, the roaring sound frightened me enough to change course again, keeping well away from this miniature tornado. The waterspout had kept a steady course, but suddenly it changed and now came towards us.

I was ready to go about, when the column of water stretching from sea to cloud seemed to get weaker, and change color from black to grey. I kept my course, and just at the moment when the spout crossed our course it disappeared. But a heavy "rainfall" of sea water fell on us containing several fish, one of which landed on top of Sam's head. The expression on his face was so marvelously funny that even Constanza could not help laughing.

"Truly a flying fish," Sam laughed as well, and picked up the fish which was still very much alive and flipping its tail in an effort to escape. "For this you deserve to live. Go and tell your friends of your adventure," he said and threw it overboard.

"Fish can't talk," I remarked as I changed course to due south.

"How do you know, maybe they can," Sam said. "Remember the Indian boy? We could not understand him, but he could talk. We just don't understand fish language." A gull flew by and gave a loud cry as it passed. "There, that bird just said something, I didn't understand it, but it spoke."

"I have a little dog at home. It often speaks to me." Constanza looked at Sam. "I don't understand everything it says, but most of it."

Sam smiled. "Dogs are easy to understand, but cats are different, they are more secretive. Dogs talk with both ends at the same time; the mouth is busy barking while the tail is as hard at work wagging."

"Even though men do not have tails to wag, I have seen them do it," I said, recalling some of the pirates' behavior in front of Blackbeard. "On board the ship that I was taken from, there was a merchant who was so frightened of Captain Teach, that every part of him spoke of his fear as plainly as his mouth that was begging for mercy."

"Did they kill him?" asked Constanza.

"No," I shook my head. "He knew my father, or rather of him. He told Captain Teach that he was rich, and so Blackbeard decided to keep me and let him go."

"Did your father pay a ransom?" Constanza asked.

"I think Blackbeard meant to ask for one. But in a way, money was not important to him. He was after something else."

"Who knows what a madman wants. He liked killing, that I am sure of." Sam looked towards the west where the sun would soon be setting. "And liked William. He called him princeling."

"Princeling," Constanza echoed.

"You know I never wanted to hear that word again." I was angry, and I looked away. But Sam went on.

"Blackbeard murdered more men than you and I and Constanza could count on our fingers and toes. I have no use for him, and I would thank the man who kills him." Sam turned towards me almost with distaste. "You think well of him merely because he did not mistreat you."

I did not know what to make of Sam's sudden anger. But I suddenly wanted to get off the boat as soon as possible. I saw a little island to the east. "Let us anchor there," I said, trying to calm myself.

I remembered the treatment the major had meted out to his son, and what had happened to Constanza in the hands of some pirate no better or worse than Blackbeard. "You are right," I admitted reluctantly. "He was a madman and a murderer, and I, too, would thank the man who kills him."

We anchored and went ashore and built a little fire on the beach, more for company than warmth. Sam and I swam, keeping a distance between us, but just as we were ready to get out we met near the water's edge. "I am sorry," Sam looked crestfallen. "I only think that you are wrong in thinking too well of him."

I nodded, still not altogether ready to forgive him for the things he said, or telling Constanza the name that Captain Teach had called me.

"I will never say it again." Sam held out his hand to me.

Finally I grabbed it, and smiling, said, "Maybe it fits me better than I care to admit."

"Oh, no, it was wrong of me to say it." Sam let go of my hand. We were still chest-deep in the sea.

"No, you were right in saying it. I am a princeling. Race you to the beach," I yelled and started swimming.

Chapter 29

The island of Cuba

A GOOD WEEK HAD PASSED SINCE WE HAD PLUN-
dered the wrecked pirate vessel. Although we were still on the
bank, I noticed that the sea was getting a deeper hue. But the
water was not yet almost bottomless as it would be if we had
reached the open ocean. That night we sailed without anchoring
and in the morning we saw a solitary rock, but by noon no islands
were in sight. I kept my course, hoping that we would reach Hispaniola or Cuba before nightfall. It was not easy to be cooped up
in a little boat, with food that was hardly edible and water that was
neither fresh nor cool. You start dreaming of all the delicous meals
that you had ever eaten, and water cool and clear from a spring.

As the sun was setting, Sam spied some small islands to the
east of us and I changed course for them. They were a small
string of low keys. We anchored near one, and luckily Sam managed to hook a fish or two, which made a meal that seemed like a
feast. There was no water on the island, but plenty of driftwood
for a fire.

"We have very little water left," Sam observed, which I knew as well.

"Tomorrow we should see the southeastern end of Cuba, or the western part of Hispaniola. Both have mountains and should be visible from afar," I declared. On my way from Jamaica I had sailed through what was called the windward passage between the two islands, and I was sure that I would recognize it again.

"We will land and get water, and maybe..." Sam grinned, "we shall be able to buy or steal a chicken. I can almost taste it now."

"Fish, though, is better than bread soaked in water." I had just finished my share of Sam's catch. We had been living on the bread we had found in the pirate ships, and they were eatable, though not very palatable, after having been soaked in water. "It is strange that when I was at home, I never thought of food. It was something that was there whenever you wanted it. But then," I added with a grin, "I was a princeling."

"In Barbados I, too, ate well. My father beat me but he never starved me. You can only appreciate what you haven't got, I guess. Though I don't think I shall ever miss the beatings," Sam laughed.

"But will we care more for food now that we know what it is like to go without it?" I asked.

"No." Sam shook his head. "For a week, maybe even a month, as you fill your belly you might recall what it was like to be hungry. But soon you will have forgotten it. Though it is a good tale to tell of pirate life, that half the time you are starving. There are no rats on board a pirate ship."

"There are no rats because there is no food for them?" Constanza asked.

"Oh no, because the pirates have eaten them." Sam poked the fire with a stick. "It is funny. The buccaneers all claim that as soon as they get gold enough, they will go ashore and live a life of ease. Yet I believe that Sir Henry Morgan is the only one who ever did it. The others will spend in three weeks what it took them half a year to gather. It is not the thirst for gold that make a pirate."

"What is it, then?" I asked. The moon had risen turning the still waters of the ocean into a sheet of silver.

"One might call it the hope of the hopeless," Sam smiled grimly. "You make a dream come true, but it is still a dream. It lacks substance. Even when your pockets are filled with stolen golden doubloons, they are not real. They are dream money and you spent them or rather threw them away in a cheap tavern in the first harbour you dare enter."

"Maybe," Sam smiled grimly, "it is the pleasure of gambling with your life that is so attractive to them. You know how they are always playing with dice or cards, and how they lose and win almost as if they do not care what happens to them. To make the stake that is the most valuable of all, your life, is the greatest wager of them all."

"Yes," I said, "that is true. That was what Blackbeard was doing, gambling with his life, and that explains why he did not really care about the money."

"All pirates are horrid," Constanza interrrupted in a childish voice.

"That they are," Sam and I both agreed, looking at the girl.

"They are bad men. I hate them." The girl sniffed and I thought she was going to cry. She was still only a child and because of that, what had happened to her was even more horrible.

"Look," Sam pointed to the sky, "there was a falling star. Let's make a wish."

"But you must not tell what you wish for," I said, as Con-stanza looked up at the sky.

"Let's sleep," I suggested, "so that we can get underway as soon as it grows light. Tomorrow we shall anchor where we can get a chicken and have a feast."

"Tomorrow, Cuba or Hispaniola, I don't care which. Chickens are alike in both places." With those words Sam stretched himself out on the sand.

We got underway before the sun rose. We had little bread and hardly any water left. What would happen to us if we were days away from the two islands? We could go without food, but we would not last long without water. I had made myself captain, and now I might have to pay for my presumption. As the little key we had anchored by disappeared, I grew increasingly worried.

By noon, the westerly breeze was light, but we were making good headway. I kept staring ahead and sometimes I believed I saw land, but then it would disappear. In the early afternoon I saw a cloud low in the horizon to the south, but I said nothing for fear it, too, would vanish. Therefore, it was Sam who got the honor of shouting "land ahead" first.

Indeed it was land. What I thought was a cloud slowly became a moutain. Was it Cuba or was it Hispaniola? Both islands were infested with pirates and robbers. It would be best for us to find an uninhabited cove, and to fill our keg and bottles with water. Once we had water on board, we could always make for the open sea should we be in danger.

The mountainous parts of Cuba and Hispaniola are the guardians of the windward passage leading to Jamaica. I had kept a course more accurate than I could have imagined in my wildest dreams. If it is possible to grow an inch or two with pride, I surely did. Sam said that if he had been the king, he would have made me a knight on the spot. "Sir William of the Windward Passage," he declared me and bowed deeply.

We talked and joked about chickens well roasted, yams and succulent fruit, and then the breeze died and we drifted a few miles from land. We soaked the last of the bread in the last of the water as the evening light dimmed and night fell. The sea was too deep now for us to anchor, so we furled the sails and waited for the wind to come back.

One of us would keep watch during the night while the others slept. Sam took the first watch, and woke me as the moon rose. The night was so still that we spoke to each other in whispers. "I think I saw light ashore," Sam pointed in the direction of land. "It was a fire, I think, but now it is gone. I believe we are drifting in an eastern direction, but I am not sure."

"East would be better than west. I think it is Cuba not Hispaniola." Vaguely, like a black shadow in the darkness, I could see the mountains.

"Tomorrow we will have chicken. And you know what is even better than that? Some clear, cool water. I shall dream about that. A pool of sweet water that I shall swim in. Goodnight." Sam lay down upon the bed we had made from the spare sail I had taken from the pirate ship, and soon he was asleep.

Alone, I sat down on the halfdeck and leaned against the mast. Suddenly I realized that in a few days I might be home, that my adventure was almost over. I thought how happy and proud my father and Mary would be, and wondered if my mother would care. Then I daydreamed foolishly about all that I would do for Sam. He would be in charge of my father's plantations and we would be friends forever.

A loud splash near the boat brought me back to reality. A dolphin circled the boat causing myriads of little lights to appear in its wake. Finally, the moon disappeared. I did not wake Sam but stayed at my post. When the eastern horizon grew light the wind came, a weak breeze from the west. I woke Sam and we got underway.

We were hungry and thirsty, and I knew that by noon when the sun had had a chance to bake us, we would truly suffer from lack of water. I steered for the coast, and we found a small cove where there were a few huts. Sam said that meant we could buy food. We took down the sails and anchored up near the shore, but far enough to require swimming. Some children appeared from one of the huts, and then a woman. She stood for a while looking at us, but then went inside again.

"I shall swim ashore," Sam announced. "If it is all right, I will call you, and if not I will try and make my way back."

"Take my sword," I suggested. Sam laughed, but he did pick up one of the dirks he had taken from the wreck and put it in his belt. Then he lowered himself over the side, and swam only a few strokes before wading ashore. Constanza and I watched him. The children did not seem frightened, and Sam talked to them. Then turning towards us he shouted, "Cuba." I had expected that it was, and that was even better than Hispaniola, because Jamaica is slightly southwest of it.

He disappeared into the hut and stayed inside so long that I began to worry. But Constanza thought that he was eating, and as it turned out, she was right. Finally he came out, made no signs for us to come ashore, and waded into the sea. I gave him a hand pulling him up.

"Is it all right?" I asked and Sam.

Sam's smile was answer enough. "Dinner will be ready in an hour. The fattest of her chickens is being roasted. There is bread, too, hot from the oven the hen has just gone into. The feast I promised."

"Is there water there?" I asked.

"Cool and clear, from a mountain stream. This is as near to heaven as I shall ever get," Sam laughed. "The man is away, which is good for us. I suspect that he may be at sea, and if he is, I am almost certain that the black flag is hoisted from the gaff of his boat."

"Let's pull the boat a little farther in, and then get water. I think it will be best to sleep on board, or maybe even pull our anchor up before night. If her husband is a pirate, he may have friends here who are no better."

"True," Sam agreed. "I don't trust her, only her cooking." With those words he jumped overboard, swam to the anchor, and dived for it. He managed to drag it in where he could stand, and the boat followed. It was not a safe anchorage should the wind come up, and I decided we would get underway as soon as we had eaten.

Since Constanza could not swim we carried her in, which we managed without getting more than her feet wet. Then we went back for our little keg and the bottles. It was a beautiful, clear stream, and we washed the salt off ourselves as soon as we had filled the keg and the flasks. We even washed our hair, not noticing that Constanza and the little girl from the hut were watching us.

When we had finished and dressed ourselves, Constanza called and said that now she wanted to wash, but that we were to go away. Sam and I declared that we did not care to watch, and carried the water on board. Then we went to the hut, and we could smell the chicken from the doorway. The woman gave me a piece of bread with oil and salt on it. It was freshly baked and tasted so delicious.

While I ate it, I suddenly recalled that I had seen a boy of about ten summers when we had first anchored up. He had been on the beach with the girl. I made a sign to Sam to follow me out-side and told him about the boy. He said he would ask the woman where the boy had gone, but I thought that was not wise, because it would be a warning that we suspected her. "We will eat and then get underway. But we will act as if we have decided to stay the night," I said, and Sam agreed.

If I live to be a hundred years old and dine with kings, I shall never eat a better meal than the one the woman served us. We ate and ate until I feared that my tummy would burst. Sam paid for our meal and we bought some yams already cooked and two loaves of bread. The woman suggested that we sleep on the bed in her hut, and it was surely tempting, but I was afraid that we might never wake from that sleep.

We told the woman that we would stay for the night, but we would sleep in the boat, and Sam even told her what we would like for breakfast. As soon as we got the food and ourselves on board, we hoisted the sails and pulled up the anchor.

We had indeed been lucky, for we were but a hundred yards from the cove when we saw four men emerge from the forest. They made motions with their hands for us to return, but only fools would have done that.

Now we followed the coast in a southeastern direction towards the Windward Passage.

Chapter 30

The Windward Passage and home

BY THE TIME IT GOT DARK WE ANCHORED FAR-
ther down the coast. The wind was dying but it would be up
again at sunrise. We kept watch but no one bothered us, and just
as I had expected, the wind came back as the sky grew light. It
had shifted a little and now came almost from the north. This
was good for us, for as soon as we hit the passage we would have
to change course to south by southwest.

A little before noon the land fell away. I had kept about a
mile from the shore, and now I changed course for Jamaica.
The sound of the name of the island made the blood rush
through my veins. I loved the island. My island. Mine? Yes,
maybe. I grinned at the thought. I would have to get used to
it, as denying it was merely foolish. I was no longer a boy, I
was a man, and that was good too. Maybe all princelings
should be captured by pirates, I thought, and smiled. Would
my father send me to England again? If he did, I would have to
go, but I would come back. Maybe there were things to learn

in England. "Bristol," I whispered, the town that Blackbeard was so proud of having come from.

I saw from the sails that the wind was almost aft. I looked at Sam. His eyes were closed. "Are you asleep?" I asked.

"I was," Sam smiled. "Do you want me to steer for a while?"

"No, I don't mind. I just wanted to ask you something."

"Yes?" Sam looked at me expectantly.

"You are my friend, aren't you? I mean, forever and ever?"

Sam laughed, and then repeated my last words, "Forever and ever."

"Will we be home soon?" Constanza asked.

I nodded. "Tomorrow, or maybe the day after."

In our part of the world a northern wind is rare. Our breezes blow mostly from the south or southeast and sometimes from the west, but hardly ever from the north. I was not surprised, therefore, when the wind died and then spun around and came from the south. It meant we had to tack. By nightfall, the wind became very light and went a little easterly, which meant that we could keep a course for Jamaica, sailing close-hauled. We had now been in our little craft for many weeks. We had enough food and good water. It really did not matter if we had to stay another day or two, but we were all eager to get to port. It was as if we could not bear to spend another day at sea.

"Tomorrow," I said as we ate our evening meal, "surely tomorrow we will be there."

"Jamaica." Sam tasted the name of the island. "I like that. It is bigger than Barbados. It was so small, there was hardly room to breathe."

"Was it as small as the place you found me?" Constanza asked very seriously, which made Sam laugh.

"Oh, it is much bigger than that. It even has a small mountain on it, or a large hill. I climbed it once."

"Is it beautiful?" Constanza frowned. "Jamaica is."

"I never thought about it." Sam looked at the red sky in the west. The sun had just set. "A place where you are unhappy can somehow never be beautiful in your eyes. But in truth, it probably is."

"I was very happy," Constanza said in a very solemn tone. "Our house was very big, and the garden was filled with flowers."

I remembered Mary cutting flowers in our garden and bringing them into the house. I closed my eyes for a minute so that I could picture my home in my mind. I opened them quickly again when I saw only my mother's room.

Neither Sam nor I slept much that night, and when dawn came we were both awake. "Can you see it?" I asked.

Sam shook his head. "Only the sea, but look how dark it has become. We must be in deep waters."

A whole school of flying fish leaped out of the water just in front of our bow. "It must be there." I pointed southwest. "We can't have missed it."

"Maybe it has disappeared like Port Royal did," Sam suggested.

I had told Sam about the great earthquake that happened some years before I was born, which caused most of the city of Port Royal to sink into the sea. My parents' house had been among those that disappeared. They had been away on one of my father's plantations. It was after that he built our house in Kingston where I had grown up.

"No, it is out there somewhere, but I shall find it." I let the mainsail out a little as the wind must have shifted a degree or two. By noon we still could not see land. I tied the tiller while we ate our midday meal. Our little boat kept its course more or less. We were sitting on the cockpit floor and Sam was telling a tale from Barbados, when suddenly our boat went into the wind and the sails began to flap. I untied the tiller and got her back on course. And there to the south I saw the peaks of the blue mountains rising above the horizon.

"Jamaica!" I shouted and pointed.

"They are tall mountains," Sam said in awe. "You might get out of breath climbing them."

"You would," I agreed, "We are seeing them from the north. On the southern coast, in the foothills, is the city of Kingston." I changed the course a little, now steering for the mountains.

"Will we get there before it gets dark?" Constanza asked anxiously.

I sighed. The girl was such a child still. "No, not tonight, but tomorrow morning for certain," I said, and Constanza climbed in under the halfdeck.

In the early morning, the sun had hardly risen when we passed the inlet to Kingston harbor. To starboard we could still see the ruins of what once had been the great town of Port Royal. The wind was light, so it took us a long time to get in. I was so happy, pointing out to Sam all the landmarks that I knew, but he was in very deep thought.

Finally, we tied up by a jetty, and I jumped ashore. Tonight I shall sleep in a bed, I thought.

I told Sam and Constanza to wait in the boat until I came back, and ran to my father's house. He had just gotten up and was drinking his morning coffee. When he saw me, the cup he held fell to the floor. He rushed to embrace me and there were tears in his eyes. I immediately told him about Sam and Constanza waiting in the boat.

He called Mary and ordered her to take me to my mother. When she came into the room and saw me, she looked as though she had seen a ghost.

My father spoke. "Hurry to your mother. There will be time to talk later." But I could not wait. Halfway up the stairs we both stopped.

"I have never stopped thinking of you, Will," she said. "Not for a moment."

"Nor I you," I answered truthfully. "Not for a moment." We laughed and taking her hand as I had done a thousand times, we passed up the stairs and through the corridor that led to my mother's room.

I stood just inside the door and Mary said, "It is William, Ma'am. He has come home."

"Are you well?" she asked and looked at me, and I wondered if she saw me, or indeed anything at all.

"Yes, mother," I answered and she looked away.

Once outside her room, Mary said, "She does not live here, but somewhere else. You must not be angry at her." I nodded to show that I understood, and she smiled and said, "I am so glad that you are back."

I really looked at Mary for the first time since I arrived. I remembered when Sam had said she must be my sister, and I had realized it might be true. Now that we were all together again, I would have many questions to ask my father.

I took my leave of Mary as my father had gotten himself ready to go to the boat with me. On the way, I told him all about Sam, and how much I liked him. I asked him if the ship that I had sailed on, the *Sarah Rose*, had come back. He said it had, and that Captain O'Rourke had told him what had happened, and had dealt with the merchant who told Blackbeard who I was. By the grimness of his answer, I did not dare ask further.

When we came to the boat, Sam was gone. Constanza was sitting alone in the cockpit. "Where is Sam?" I asked, surprised.

"He has gone," The girl said, and then rose and curtsied to my father. My father bowed to her.

"Where has he gone?" I shouted, and my father put his hand on my shoulder.

"He said he was going to the mountains and that you would understand." Constanza was near tears. "I told him to wait for you, but he said he could not."

I had told Sam about the mountains, and he had gone there. I understood, and yet I felt betrayed. All my dreams were only dreams, after all. My friend had left me and I was alone.

"Come," my father said, taking Constanza's hand and helping her up the pier. I looked at him and then at the girl. "He was my friend," I whispered.

"I am sure he still is," my father said, looking back to the mountains rising beyond the city. "Some day he will come back."

I, too, looked towards the mountains and then repeated my father's words. "Some day he will come back." And then I felt better for I knew that it was true, and that Sam and I would be friends forever and ever.

My father put his arm around my shoulders, and with Constanza, we turned towards home.

Epilogue

I HAD BEEN HOME BUT A FEW MONTHS WHEN news arrived in Jamaica of the death of Captain Teach. Anchored on his sloop near Ocracoke Inlet, he was attacked by two vessels commanded by a Lieutenant Robert Maynard. Blackbeard died in the battle with 25 wounds to his body and his head was attached to the bowsprit of Maynard's vessel. Many of his men died with him, among them Gibbens, Roberts the carpenter, and John Husk. I was glad that John lost his life in that fight, for I could not bear the thought of him being hanged. Of the pirates who were captured, most ended their lives at the end of a rope. Isreal Hands was pardoned and Sam Odell was acquitted. Why those two rascals escaped I do not know, but justice is often blind.

Sam's father, Major Bonnet was caught, as his son had foretold. He died not bravely but true to his nature. Crying and begging for mercy, cursing grandfather Peachell whom he thought was the cause of his fate, he was dragged to the gallows.

Constanza was reunited with her family, prominent Spanish landowners, and went to live with relatives of her mother.